The Search for South Pole Santa

A Christmas Adventure

BY

JingleBelle Jackson

ISBN: 1479263559
ISBN 13: 9781479263554
CreateSpace, North Charleston, SC

For my nephews, most of all, who inspired this story

Tyler

Nathan

Spencer

And for,

my husband, Glen, who is my biggest fan

my parents, who have always believed in me

my sisters, brothers-in-law and nieces, who cheer me on

my tiniest niece Savanna who will always be on Santa's good list

PROLOGUE

An Alarming Sound

Location: The North Pole, present day

Clang! Clang! Clang!

Alert ! Alert !

Bongo! Bongo!

Rum A Dum!

Bango! Bango!

Oooga! Oooga!

Alert ! Alert !

Chapter 1

Hubbub at the Pole

Location: Present Day at the North Pole

"We interrupt this broadcast for breaking news from the North Pole. Yes, that North Pole," the reporter dressed in a crisp white shirt, heavy suit jacket and black slacks said, speaking into her microphone as she quickly walked up a sidewalk lined with oversized candy canes. At a magnificent front door, made of ornate wood and very old stained glass, she rang the bell and heard a chorus of "*...deck the halls with boughs of holly...,*" which turned her stern look into a smile. "In an unprecedented first, Santa Claus has called a press conference with important news for the world," she continued, now serious again, as the door opened."We turn now to Mr. Claus. Sir, may I call you Santa?"

"Ho Ho Ho! Of course! Everyone does. Hello children! Can you see me?" said the man people all around the world know as Santa Claus, who then stepped out the door and tapped on the camera's lens.

The view cut to another camera for a moment to show Santa was standing in front of his own front door at the North Pole.

Through the centuries, Santa's house had always impressed those who got to see it and this time was no exception. It was rare to get a glimpse of how Santa lived. The house had been built in the same whimsical style as most homes at the Pole with a large, over-sized sloping roof made to carry a heavy snow load. The outside was painted in bright multi-colored hues of colors that sparkled even on cloudy days. Christmas lights adorned the home year-round, and the front windows were shaped like Christmas tree ornaments complete with festive matching shutters.

The reporter held the microphone close to Santa but it was unnecessary. He spoke in a loud, booming voice. "I wanted to speak with all of you in TV land today to share some important news about a slight problem that has come up here at the Pole. Well, around the world actually.

"Our population alarm has sounded. Now that probably doesn't mean much to any of you, but as you look around your towns and cities, you may notice that there are more children than ever. I bet some of you may even have a new baby brother or sister!" Santa smiled and paused before he continued.

"I love children! The babies, the little ones, the big ones, the good ones – even you naughty ones," Santa said wagging his finger slightly at the camera. "And surely all of you know that our goal here at the North Pole is to make certain each and every child in the world receives a special gift with no exception."

"Is that in jeopardy, Santa?" the reporter cut in with concern in her voice.

"Well yes," Santa replied directly but had to pause as an audible gasp was heard from the reporter – and in every home watching the news cast as well! "I know, I know," he continued, hurriedly responding to her reaction and anticipating the rest of the world would feel the same. "This is a bit of a shock to take in when you first hear it, and we here at the North Pole heard it very loud." He chuckled at his little joke about the loud alarm, putting his hands over his ears briefly, remembering the volume of the alert.

"When the population alarm sounded, it did exactly what it was set to do hundreds of years ago – alert us if we ever approached having too many children for Santa to serve. Certainly, we hoped this day would never come. Thinking about it now, perhaps we should have anticipated this, but here at the Pole our focus is always on the children," he paused looking a bit pensive. "However, after a week of careful consideration, evaluating the situation and putting our best minds on the problem, I am very pleased to share that we have quickly come up with a solution to this predicament. That is why I called for this TV coverage today."

"Santa, please continue. I know our viewers, especially the children, are anxious to hear more," said the reporter.

"In the end, the answer was simple. We have too many children for *one* Santa to serve," and he made sure to stress the word *one*. "So we simply need to add a second Santa. There's no getting around it and we begin the search today."

"A second Santa?" the reporter sputtered. "But who? Who could be you?"

"Now that is an excellent question and the answer is that many people could be. In fact, this presents a very unique opportunity for someone who has always dreamed of being Santa. But we only have room for one. After all, I'm already here and not going any place," Santa said, laughing at his own comment.

"If there are so many people, how do you plan to select the right person to be another you?"

"Ho Ho Ho! Well since children have been writing to Santa for centuries, it seems only right that becoming Santa should involve a letter, too," Santa answered. "After much consideration, in consultation with the North Pole Claus Council, we have determined that interested individuals need only be Santa Believers, over sixteen human years of age, and send us a letter outlining why he or she wants to be Santa." He got close to the camera lens again and added, "Speak from your heart.

"And one more thing, there's no time to waste! We need your letters to arrive here at the North Pole within one week!"

"One week!" said the reporter, obviously stunned by the fast turnaround. "With all due respect, Mr. Claus, isn't that short time-frame a little unreasonable?"

"Ho Ho Ho! Maybe for some, maybe for some," he agreed, shaking his head. "But this person will be delivering gifts to children all around the world in the span of one magical night every year. They will need to be comfortable with – and good at – working fast! Ho Ho Ho! There's no time to waste! Get your pens and pencils out and start writing."

Word of the announcement would make its way around the world to places near and far, including a very hard-to-find island somewhere in a remote part of the Caribbean. It was there on St. Annalise Island that Cassandra Penelope Clausmonetsiamlydelaterra…, Sandra for short, and her guardian Captain Richmond, affectionately called Cappie by most, had come to live six years ago. Their time on the island had been happy but their reason for being there had come about through tragedy.

Chapter 2

Sandra and Cappie

Location: Somewhere in the South Pacific Six Years Ago

For months, Cappie had been worried sick about eleven-year-old Sandra. Her parents, Cassiopola and Sanderson – Cassy and Sandy – had gone missing one calm day while Sandra and Cappie were busy with errands on a local island. Word of the loss spread through the South Pacific Islands they were calling home at the time, but no one came forward with any information. Weeks of searching had turned up absolutely no sign of the couple, and local officials had declared them lost at sea. Sandra had been inconsolable over the tragic loss and unreasonable. Cappie had been trying to convince her young charge for weeks to do the one thing she refused to do – leave where they were and start new somewhere else.

"I won't leave here, Cappie. I just can't. What if my parents need our help? What will they think if they come back and we're gone? They won't know where to find us or where to even look. I'm staying here and nothing you can say will change my mind." She stomped her foot and burst into tears.

Cappie took her hand. "I hate to see you hurting so much, sweetheart, but you know they would want you to get on with your life. We both know your education was important to them, and they wanted you to enroll at an actual school for the rest of your schooling."

Cappie knew that Sandra hadn't accepted the fact that her parents were gone for good. If they had been simply lost and alive, they would have found some way to get word to their daughter by now. Over the last few months, Cappie had tried desperately to come up with the words to help Sandra accept the tragedy and had failed miserably. Now, as she stood holding Sandra's hands she tried again.

"There were so many places they wanted you to see and new experiences they wanted you to have," she said. "Your parents were special people, Sandra, and they would want you to get on with your life and fill it again with joy. They wouldn't want you to stay here and wait for them because, well, because they aren't coming back and you know they aren't." *There*, she thought, *I've said it*.

Sandra shook off Cappie's hands and faced her angrily. She might have been young but she could be formidable and stubborn. "I won't leave here, Cappie. I'm not going anywhere! I don't care at all about a new school. I'm going to be here for my parents when they come back, which I know they'll do no matter what you say!"

With that she stormed off to her room.

The two called home a tugboat named the *Mistletoe*. Sandra would lie on her bunk for hours plotting how she would get ashore and run away if Cappie decided they were leaving.

Cappie had been hired by Sandra's parents as the captain of the boat, but she had also been like a grandmother to Sandra. When Sandy and Cassy had asked her to be their daughter's guardian if anything ever happened to them, she had accepted immediately. She was determined to do what they would have wanted her to do for Sandra. At the same time, she understood the complete despair that Sandra felt. She, too, missed the couple immensely.

Sandra continued her homeschooling on board the *Mistletoe*, though Cappie knew her heart wasn't in it. She was so unlike the happy, bubbly girl she always had been that it concerned Cappie deeply. Most days Sandra was quiet now with frequent bursts of tears. The only way Cappie could still get a smile from her was to cook up one of her mother's best dishes. One evening, after another long, quiet day, she decided to surprise Sandra with her one of favorite dinners – fish tacos and pineapple slices with coconut pudding for dessert.

She set up a picnic table outside, singing to herself as she did. Her goal was to see a smile on Sandra's face again, and she thought that if she herself was in a happier mood, it might help.

Cappie looked down the deck to see Sandra sitting quietly at the back, staring out to sea. As usual, for most of the day Sandra's pet parrot Squawk was with her. Squawk was a smart bird with fancy feathers in all sorts of bright colors, especially red. When he wasn't with Sandra, the confident parrot loved to stand in front of Sandra's bedroom mirror, preening and squawking about what a good-looking bird he was.

Although Sandra's mother was elfin and, like all full elfins, had magical abilities, she had rarely used them. Since they had often been on long trips in the middle of the ocean, with no real chances for her little girl to make new friends, Cassy had made one exception, however. She had used magic to give Squawk the gift of human language and understanding, and, as Cassy had hoped, the little girl and bright parrot had become immediate friends. What was even more impressive was that Squawk, like Sandra, was multi-lingual. They both spoke English, French, Spanish, several Indonesian dialects and Mandarin Chinese. They could also understand dolphins, whales and a couple of sea bird languages. When they were outside together in nature, it was both amusing and educational to listen to them interpret what the birds were saying. On this day, they were practicing their Mandarin and Cappie had overheard her name as she walked down to where the two sat on deck.

"squawk... she's worried...squawk," Squawk said to Sandra in Mandarin.

"What are the two of you keeping from me?" Cappie asked.

"Nothing – just that you worry too much," Sandra responded in Mandarin, without thinking, before repeating it in English. She breathed in deeply. "What smells so good? All of a sudden I'm really hungry."

"I came to get you two. Dinner is served," Cappie said as Squawk flew ahead to the table.

"squawk... pretty table," Squawk said. He turned his beak towards the picnic table. "squawk... looks great... squawk"

"Thank you, Squawk," Cappie said.

Twenty minutes later the trio was already finishing up dinner. Sandra was chomping down the last of her tacos and licking her lips between bites on her juicy pineapple slices.

"This is great, Cappie."

She munched the last bite of pineapple and then finished her dinner with two helpings of the coconut pudding – with a little help from Squawk. Cappie smiled as she watched them.

"Let's go and say hello to Rio," Cappie said when they were all finished. "I saw her up by the bow a little while ago."

Before Cappie completed the sentence, Sandra was running to the front of the boat, waving at Rio who was making all kinds of noises. Rio was a bottlenose dolphin, another of Sandra's special animal friends, but not a pet. She was with them by choice and came and went as she pleased. Unlike Squawk, she wasn't enchanted. Rio was special in a striking way though – she wasn't grey or blue like most dolphins instead she was a stunning emerald green color. Sandra thought she was one of the most beautiful creatures she had ever seen. Squawk thought she had nothing on him.

Sandra and Rio touched noses before Sandra felt a slight breeze and knew that Squawk had landed beside her.

"squawk… she missed us," Squawk said to Sandra.

"I know. I missed her too. Rio, don't be gone so much," Sandra said to her favorite dolphin.

Cappie loved that Sandra had her animal friends but she often wished, especially now with her parents gone, that she had other children to play with as well. Sandra had always lived on the *Mistletoe* and been homeschooled. Her parents had been committed to exposing their daughter to different cultures. Even when Sandra was a tiny babe in arms, the family had travelled the world. Sandy and Cassy had considered themselves "worldologists" – people who studied the world. They felt they belonged to everywhere and nowhere. It was that belief that had lead to the family's very long last name. Each time they left a country they had lived in and loved, they honored it by adding a word part on to their own original last name. After living off the coast of France, they added "monet." Leaving Thailand, they chose "siam." Departing Vietnam they chose "ly" and after spending several years in several countries of Latin America they added on "de la terra." Over time, Claus had become Clausmonetsiamlydelaterra... They knew some people found it odd but it made no difference to the happy little family. To make it easier for others, they still used Claus… as a quick, shortened version. All in all, despite not knowing many other children, it was a wonderful way for Sandra to grow up and, until the recent tragedy, she had always been happy. Cappie knew, though, that Cassy and Sandy had been planning to stay put somewhere soon so Sandra could spend time attending a regular school. *But where?* she thought again. *And how would she get Sandra to go?*

Chapter 3

An Unexpected Message

Location: Somewhere in the South Pacific

Each morning on the *Mistletoe*, Sandra would do her school work and each afternoon she and Cappie would head out fruitlessly searching for her parents. She had asked Squawk and Rio, of course, if they knew anything about what happened to them, but neither of the loyal friends had been able to uncover any helpful information. It was a miserable mystery for everyone.

Just like before her parents disappeared, living on the *Mistletoe* was a comfort to Sandra. The *Mistletoe* was a 48-foot, ocean-going tugboat with three deck levels. Its coloring matched its Christmas-related name with red and white being the main colors and touches of a deep evergreen color here and there. The lowest level had plenty of space for storage in addition to the engine room. It was a loud part of the boat and no one ever stayed down there long. On the main level, there was deck space on all sides with a large back deck. Inside you could find Sandra's berth (as bedrooms are called on a boat), her parent's berth, an extra berth for guests, a general living space and the kitchen area. On the top level was the pilot room and directly behind that was Cappie's berth.

Sandra had always slept well on their comfortable tug. Most nights, the gentle rocking helped lull her to sleep. Since her parents had gone missing though, as often as not, she would spend part of her night out on deck, lying on her back watching the stars, unable to sleep despite being exhausted.

One moonlit night as she was star-gazing laying there, flat on the deck, awake and longing for her parents, she was annoyed by the sound of something banging against the side of the boat. Not a loud bang, just a simple thump, thump whenever the water moved on the starboard side. Someone who hadn't lived on a boat all their life might not have noticed it at all. In fact, when Sandra first heard it, she thought it might be Rio. The busy dolphin usually chose to rest at night so that would have been unusual. She knew it wasn't Squawk either since she could hear him snoring through the open window of her berth. After awhile, it didn't matter that she didn't know who or what it was. What she did know was that it was annoying – like someone tapping their pen against a hard surface over and over. She pushed herself up from where she had plopped on deck, and went over to toss what she was sure was driftwood or sea junk onto the boat to get rid of later.

The full moon made it easy for her to spot the guilty noise-maker – a bottle. She hated sea garbage. She reached down with a net and scooped the bottle up on deck with barely a glance. As she did, however, the moonlight reflected off it and something caught her eye. Instead of just dumping it in the trash, she took a closer look.

The bottle had no label. Instead, it had something better. There was a rolled up piece of paper inside it! *A message in a bottle?* she thought, her curiosity immediately triggered. Thoughts were racing through her head. She had heard about messages in bottles but she never thought she'd actually find one. Maybe she could write back. They could be pen pals and she could use a new friend right about now.

The moon was full and bright enough that she didn't need any additional light to see. The bottle was small and had a cork in it rather than any screw-type lid but the message looked dry. She tugged on the cork and had to twist on it hard before it gave way. She poked her index finger in as far as it would reach and managed to twist the paper just enough to make it fit through the opening. She unwound it and read the very short message:

Go to St. Annalise Island
Go to St. Annalise Island

Sandra jumped back, dropping the paper to the deck. *What was this?* she thought, her mind racing with questions. *What kind of trick was someone playing? Who sent this? How did it get here?* She grabbed it up and read it again.

Go to St. Annalise Island
Go to St. Annalise Island

The ink sparkled in the moonlight. Unbelievably, she knew who had written it. In fact, she knew with certainty that she was staring at her mother's writing. She ran below to wake up Cappie. They had to get going. Her parents were alive!

She knew it.

"CAPPIE!"

Chapter 4

Go or No Go

Location: On the Mistletoe somewhere in the South Pacific

Cappie was not as convinced as Sandra. It had been months. If they were alive, why hadn't they contacted them? If they did send the message, why was it so short and stuck in a bottle, for goodness sake? Why not just pick up the radio? Maybe write them a letter? She had so many questions! *Or c'mon, just show up in person,* she thought frustratingly.

At the same time, it did look like Cassy's writing and it did have the family emblem on it. When Sandra was an infant, Cassy and Sandy had created a simple emblem to represent their small family. It was three straight lines in a circle. The lines represented the three of them and the circle represented the world they were exploring and living on. As far as Cappie knew, no one else knew about that.

The questions continued to roll through her mind. Like, why, if the couple was alive, didn't they just say so? Were they being held somewhere? Were they on this St. Annalise Island? If not, what was on St. Annalise? Where was St. Annalise? If only she had as many answers as she did questions. Sandra, on the other hand, was sure her parents were on St. Annalise and just wanted to get going.

Before that could happen, Cappie decided, the first thing they needed to do was find this St. Annalise Island on a map. So they headed to the big map hanging on the wall in the galley (which is a kitchen for anyone not living on a boat) and the two began looking. It didn't take long because St. Annalise turned out to be one of the places that Cassy and Sandy had circled at some point. St. Annalise was a tiny spot on the map in the southern part of the Caribbean Sea.

"Let's go!" said Sandra, jumping up and down and dancing around enough to knock over a big pitcher of water that was sitting on the table. "Let's pack up and set sail first thing tomorrow! I'm sure mom and dad are there!" Sandra was like a completely different child then she had been for months and, while Cappie welcomed the change, it was fast and drastic.

"Sandra, first, we, meaning you, young lady, need to clean up this water mess you've made." Sandra had already reached for a rag, knowing she would indeed be expected to clean it up. "Then, we need to be sure that's what we want to do and where we want to go. It's about as far away from here as anywhere we could have selected to go. Even if that's what we decide, we can't possibly leave tomorrow because we need to get supplies, make some arrangements, contact people – it's going to take a couple of days at best. Did you ever hear your parents talk about that island or a school being there?"

Sandra shook her head. "No, I don't think so. Or maybe. I'm not really sure."

Cappie picked up the big box of travel and school brochures from a corner in the galley that Sandra's parents had been collecting and plopped it next to Sandra. "Give a look in here and see if you can find out anything about the island. Let's start there. And be careful that you don't get any of them soaked. Look, there's still water there," as she pointed to a small puddle on the far end of the table. "Maybe when we've glanced through them before, we just never noticed one was on this St. Annalise."

Chapter 5

Finally An Answer

Location: On the Mistletoe somewhere in the South Pacific

Sandra had been at it more than an hour and gone through about half the box when she stopped to take a break. "Nothing. I can't find a thing. Nothing at all."

"If there's nothing there, why would they want us to go?" Cappie shook her head as Sandra went back to rummaging in the box. "It doesn't make sense. They always –"

"Here! This one! This school is on St Annalise!" Sandra was waving a plain-looking folder in the air. She sat down next to Cappie, opened it to a brochure inside, and they both began to read.

The St Annalise Academy

At the St Annalise Academy, our students attend classes in one of the most beautiful, intimate settings in the world. St Annalise has offered students a unique learning experience for more than 300 years. Your child will study topics to help him or her negotiate the world as it is and contribute to making it better. We offer academic subjects (as well as some that are a bit light-hearted). Our commitment is to prepare your unique child for the world he or she will live in after graduating from St Annalise.

Our philosophy

We believe each day should be lived joyfully. Our view is that even in some of the most difficult situations, those times when the world is in chaos or sadness comes to our lives, we can each choose to find goodness and moments of hope. We encourage our students to seek out fun and to laugh out loud as often as possible.

Topics offered at St Annalise include:

Lost languages
Physics and quantum physics
Present-day cultures/History of lost cultures
Meditation
Ethical dilemmas
Animal behavior/Animal languages
Ocean exploration
Inner exploration
Geography of the top world
International cooking & baking
Child behavior
World finance systems
Nutrition
Costuming & fashion

In addition, each day at St. Annalise includes an emphasis on sports and wellness activities. Our current curriculum includes lessons in:

Deepwater diving
Fencing
Tai chi/yoga
Surfing
Circus acrobatics/gymnastics
Strategy games
Flying

Upon graduation, your child will have an appreciation for the world we share from many different perspectives. We welcome humans, elves, elfins, leprechauns, gnomes, moonrakers, talleehos, wizards and fairies. *All attendees must be Santa Believers.* (We also allow brownies and trolls with prior permission.)

Our graduates have gone on to prominent visible positions of power worldwide and to quiet positions that have changed history and left mysteries.

The two finished reading the brochure and then unfolded a sheet of paper also in the folder. It read:

Dearest Sanderson and Cassiopola
Clausmonetsiamlydelaterra...,

It is with great pleasure that we share with you that your daughter, Cassandra, has been accepted to attend the St. Annalise Academy. The starting date is enclosed. We recommend that you arrive prior to that date to become acquainted with the island and allow Sandra time to attend orientation.

Further information about St. Annalise Academy is enclosed. We are confident you will find no better education available top world to suit your daughter. I look forward to personally welcoming her.

Most sincerely,

Christina Annalise

Christina Annalise
Academy Director & Headmistress

"Christina Annalise of St Annalise Island and St. Annalise Academy?" said Sandra repeating what they had just read. "Is she the owner of the island and the school?" Cappie just shrugged. It didn't really matter. By the time they had finished reading the letter, they were both convinced that St. Annalise Island was indeed where they were supposed to be headed.

Chapter 6

On Their Way

Location: On the Mistletoe somewhere at sea

The term start date was just weeks away. By the next evening, Sandra and Cappie had bought supplies and said their quick goodbyes. They shared the specific information on where they were going with two friends on the closest island, just in case Sandra's parents showed up looking for them. Most notable, however, they didn't mention the bottle message. The two had agreed not to tell anyone about it. If it was some kind of trick, or a strange, random note in a bottle, then it didn't matter whether they talked about it or not. On the other hand, if it really was a message from Cassy and Sandy, then it meant that not only were they possibly alive, they could be in some kind of danger. A part of both Sandra and Cappie wanted to stay to continue their search, but their hearts – and the message – told them to go.

They also stopped to send a letter by special air delivery to the academy since there was no email address or phone number listed anywhere in the brochure and they didn't know if Cassy and Sandy had let Christina Annalise know Sandra would be enrolling. The duo, plus Squawk, and Rio swimming along, set sail for St. Annalise by late afternoon.

Once they were underway, Sandra had time to study the brochure in more detail and Cappie studied the map. They had sailed long distances many times before and were at ease at sea, but this was the first time they had sailed without Cassy and Sandy. Cappie felt the added responsibility of making certain that Sandra was safe and well. Now that they were underway and headed to the island, both felt a calm they had not had since the day of the couple's disappearance months ago. They were full of happy anticipation about their new home.

"What does Christina Annalise mean when she says 'top world' Cappie?"

"That's a good question. Legend has it we live on a hollow Earth and a totally different world is happening inside our planet. It might be so or it might not. Personally, I haven't ever known anyone from that world that I know of, but that doesn't mean it doesn't exist. Maybe that's what she means," said Cappie in response.

"Okay, wow. How do you even get there? Oh, never mind. I know you don't know either. How many students do you think go to St Annalise, Cappie?" she asked changing the subject completely.

"It doesn't say but it looks to be a fairly small school."

"I think it's a boarding school, but I want to be sure and stay on the *Mistletoe*."

"We'll talk to them about that when we get there."

Chapter 7

St. Annalise!

Location: St. Annalise somewhere in the Caribbean Sea

Christina Annalise herself had greeted them dockside the day they finally arrived. She was a striking woman, trim with dark hair and wore large sunglasses. Sandra would learn through the years that, except for after dark, she rarely took them off – whether she was inside or out in the bright sun. It had been a long voyage, and both Sandra and Cappie were beyond excited about getting to the island. The chance that Sandra's parents were there was a hope they had kept alive the whole trip.

The headmistress was puzzled by the idea. "I've met your parents Sandra," she had said warmly. "A very lovely couple. I was so sorry to hear they were lost at sea, but I don't recall a time they were ever here at St. Annalise."

For Sandra, this was crushing news. After the bottle message, she was sure she would find them at St. Annalise. Despite that setback, however, the lush, remote island had a magic about it, and it didn't take long for both Sandra and Cappie to feel at home. Before long, the disappointment over her parents not being there started to fade and Sandra was finally moving back to her happy self. She felt her parents wanted her there and that helped her accept them being gone. She was smiling, humming, even singing out loud at times again, with a lightness in her step that brought joy back to Cappie as well and relief that they had, indeed, found a perfect place to live.

Sandra loved everything about her new island home. To her, it had adventures waiting everywhere to be discovered. She especially loved the old school. "It's kind of mysterious, don't you think, Cappie?" Sandra asked. Cappie just listened, figuring that Sandra's young imagination had gone into high gear again. It seemed like a regular old building to her.

But the St. Annalise Academy was hardly housed in a "regular old building." The Academy was located in the 400-year-old Annalise family mansion. Long ago, the story went, Samuel Annalise was on the run and had reasons to leave England quickly. Somehow he ended up in the Caribbean where he claimed the island, named it after his family, and built the huge, sprawling mansion. Eventually, the family chose to turn the small castle-like home into St. Annalise Academy, and it was still run by descendants of Samuel Annalise.

Sandra didn't care how the mansion got there, she was just glad it was there. She had decided that it felt like home because it once was a home. It certainly didn't look like anything else on the private island, probably like nothing else in the whole of the Caribbean. Rather, it looked like an old mansion you would find in the English countryside – complete with a brick facade and two turret towers on each end of the school. No ivy, though. Instead the school was covered with climbing vines, bursting with fragrant, tropical flowers. The academy had three floors plus a basement and two turret rooms that stood above the rest. Nobody seemed to know exactly how many rooms there actually were at the school, but Sandra discovered new ones every year.

While Sandra lived on the *Mistletoe* with Cappie and Squawk, most students at the school lived in the dorm rooms on the school's third floor. Classrooms were on the second floor. On the main floor was a large hall that was originally designed to be the ballroom, cafeteria, school offices, gym, locker rooms, auditorium, student lounge area and a long hall of classrooms. The library was also on the main floor – and the second and third floors, too. It was home to hundreds of rare books that any collector or librarian would envy. Sandra loved being in the library the most. She had a favorite corner on the third-floor level that looked out at the sea where she would cuddle up with a book for hours on rare cloudy days.

St. Annalise Academy was a private school on a private island. By design, it had limited access to the outside world despite being part of a world fully using the Internet, cell phones, texting and Skype. They didn't even have newspapers or TV on the island! Christina Annalise explained it as wanting students to keep attention on their classes and the many different things the island had to offer. The rest of the world could wait till later. They had all their lives to be grown-up, she would say, when students would again implore her about being more connected. They could worry on things, explore other places, watch TV shows if they really wanted to (she couldn't imagine why) and all such stuff then. This time was about fully experiencing the here and now and living a life focused on the magic of childhood and learning.

Despite the fact that students could attend St. Annalise Academy by invitation only, everyone at the school, whether human, fairy, elfin, gnome, or something else completely, (although all looked primarily human), all believed in Santa and the magic of Christmas. Making things even more interesting, most students, being at least half something else and not human only, were gifted with some special magical skills, abilities, powers or senses as well. It all made life on the island, as far as Sandra was concerned, a whole lot of fun most of the time.

What made things the most fun for Sandra, though, had nothing to do with classes, or homework, or magic, or even her favorite sport, surfing. The best part of St. Annalise, for her, was her two best friends. Sandra had met Ambyrdena "Birdie" Snow and Spencer Mantle her first year on the island. The three had been assigned to be a team in their science exploration class together, and they had been pretty much inseparable since.

Birdie was from Africa and was the only daughter of an African princess and a water wizard father. She was slender with cocoa-colored skin and the translucent blue eyes of most water wizards. Like Sandra, she had a ready smile though she tended to be quieter than her outgoing friend. Sandra loved to hear her tell stories about Africa and what it was like to be the daughter of a princess.

"Africa is a beautiful place of contrasts," Birdie told her, when they first met, with a sophistication not seen in most children. "It's not like here on St. Annalise where we have so many different colors of green and different kinds of flowers.

At home, you can find tangled jungles with exotic animals and exotic plants right next to deserts with nothing but brown sand for miles and miles. I'm not sure where I like living better, but I think we have more birds over there." That was important to Ambyrdena since she had the special ability of talking to all kinds of birds. It wasn't actually that uncommon of an ability at St. Annalise, but Birdie was the best at it. She and Squawk would sometimes get in big arguments over what one bird or another had to say.

"You and Squawk are so funny when you fight!" said Sandra. "He says you must just make up some of the things from the other birds because he can barely understand a word the birds from here are saying at times – especially the hummingbirds."

"He's just jealous because I speak better bird then he does and he's a bird!" laughed Birdie. "He needs to work on learning more of his own species' dialects. Just because he's a parrot doesn't mean he can possibly understand everything an albatross is saying without studying the differences once in awhile. A little bit of homework would do him good!"

Spencer looked up from his notepad where he was running another set of calculations. He pushed his shaggy, sun-bleached blond hair out of the way of his dark brown eyes and snickered. "I guess the two of you must find me totally boring since I'm just 100% human. No other species in my DNA."

Sandra patted his hand. "You poor thing," she cooed.

Spencer may have wished he had some other species as part of his cellular makeup but being only human didn't keep him from being a boy genius. That was a gift at least as powerful as magic. Just entering his teens, he was already starting to publish papers unraveling some of the mysteries of DNA. As they grew up on the island, his increasingly complex work would lead to assistance with halting genetic diseases and that was before they even graduated! Spence was one of the few on the island that Christina Annalise gave permission to travel periodically to a nearby island that had Internet available. So much of his work depended on having access to vast amounts of research that it was necessary for him to be connected. He didn't abuse the privilege and had never even considered "surfing" the Net. His focus was strictly on his research. Spencer's parents were both professors at St. Annalise, so literally everyone he cared about lived right there on the island. Even as they all got older, and he posted his research findings more often, most the world only knew him by his code name "Pencil." He had no interest in the problems, or even the glory, that came with fame.

At times he could be quite the obnoxious, know-it-all. When he behaved that way, for some reason, he annoyed Sandra more than anyone else. "You don't know everything" she would tell him, knowing at the same time that he probably did. Most the time, though, like Birdie, he was the best friend she could ever want, being both loyal and supportive. He was a great listener and always gave thoughtful answers to questions. Plus, he loved to read and whenever the girls would get into "girl talk," he'd just tune them out by getting into one of his books or working on one of his new theories.

He annoyed her at times, but even Sandra would say that Spencer wasn't that bad that often. Oh no. Through the years there on St. Annalise, by far, the most irritating person to Sandra on the island was Jason Annalise. She was ridiculously drawn to the tanned classmate, but it seemed he barely knew she existed. Nonetheless, she found herself watching him whenever he was anywhere around.

"Stop making eyes at Jason," Spencer would say. "It's too much to watch."

Sandra would give him a hard punch in the arm. "You are so totally annoying me. Go away!"

"Why? So you can be alone with Jason?"

Birdie would roll her eyes, Spencer would rub his arm, and Sandra would glance again over to wherever Jason was hanging out.

Chapter 8

Jason

Location: St. Annalise Island, present day

Sandra had been interested in Jason Annalise since they first came to the island. She was not even a teen yet at that point and had a horrible crush on the boy her own age. They were feelings that were definitely not returned – not then or now. She hated that her friends could tell and hoped he couldn't. She doubted it. The vast majority of the time he seemed uninterested in almost everything – including her. Jason Annalise was tall, dark, athletic and. . .impossible!

At least that's how Sandra felt. He had a few casual friends, but he kept to himself most of the time and often acted like no one else existed. Overall, he was a mediocre student in most subjects but the best athlete on the island. Except maybe for Sandra. Sandra was strong and fit and skilled at almost every board sport. It didn't matter if it was surfing, kite boarding, sand boarding, skate boarding, even snowboarding, she loved them all! She was good at other things as well, like beach volleyball and soccer where her long, strong, legs helped give her an advantage. But if a sport came with a board, she knew she could do it. She felt like she balanced better on a board than walking, almost like she could manipulate gravity.

Every year, the island would get hit with oversized waves during a couple weeks in early October. It had something to do with wind factors, El Nino and a bunch of other things few of the students cared about except that it combined to bring in the best surfing waves of the year. It was also the biggest annual competition for the students. Growing up on an island made for a lot of great surfers, and taking the trophy at the Annalise Water Walkers competition was coveted by everyone. Jason Annalise had won it every year Sandra had been on the island. Except one. That year, two years ago when they were both almost sixteen, Sandra had caught the best wave of the day. It was a monster that she had worked like a master. She had jumped up and down, screaming, at the end of the day when the judges posted the scores. She won! She beat out everyone else and most especially Jason - the best of the best. She still smiled thinking about that fun day. It came at a cost, though. That win, it seemed to her, had sealed Jason Annalise's dislike for her since the day she took the trophy.

In fact, most of the time, Jason was one of those guys who just seemed to get in his own way. Despite all his potential and opportunity, he had a chip on his shoulder that he alone had put there. He felt like he was different from everyone else and seemed determined to make sure nobody forgot it – even though none of them ever remembered.

Unlike the other students, Jason had not been invited to St. Annalise. He was the one exception. He had actually arrived in a far more unique and special way: he had floated in lying at the bottom of a rickety dinghy. There was a note, written in Spanish, pinned to the blanket he had been placed on.

"Por favor, cuide a mi bebé. Su nombre es Jason. Tiene ocho meses. Él es mi corazón. Consientalo como a mi me gustaría hacerlo." (In English it read: *"Please take care of my baby. His name is Jason. He is eight months old. He is my heart. Cherish him as I wanted to."*)

There was no signature on the note or indicator of where he had come from. Christina Annalise took him in and immediately launched a search for his parents throughout the Caribbean. When, after two long years, no one had claimed him or come forward – much to her relief since she had loved him from the moment he floated in to their shore – she formally adopted him.

Naturally, living on the same small island and having been in many classes together, Jason and Sandra had had opportunities to talk and interact. When she thought back, though, she realized there really hadn't been very many conversations between them. He had turned her down the one time she had gotten up the nerve to ask him to a school dance. It had been painful and awkward, and afterward she felt like she might need to move from the island so she wouldn't ever see him again.

She had impulsively asked him shortly after her big Water Walkers win. Toward the end of a long day of surfing, they had both caught one of the best waves of the day and had walked out of the water, boards under their arms, together. He had been unguarded, smiling, even laughed with her about Rio riding the wave in next to them. "Great job," he said to her with what had seemed at the time to be a little bit of affectionate admiration. Together with that rare smile he flashed, she had felt good, like something had changed between them, and she went for the invitation.

"Any chance you'd like to talk more about this wave at the Annalise Lidohop?" she had asked shyly. It was the annual, traditional, girls' ask-a-date event.

He had just stared at her for a minute as she began to wish it would get dark and a sinkhole would open in the sand and bury her. Or a rogue wave would come crashing to shore and sweep her out to sea. As she longed for a disaster of any sort to take her away from the agonizingly awkward moment, for just an instant, it didn't seem quite so bad. She caught a look from him that made her think he actually was going to say "yes" – right before he blurted out "no."

"I'm going sailing," he had said. "It's what I do."

"Okay," she said embarrassed. "I just thought I'd ask. I mean now that I think of it, do you even know how to dance?" It wasn't very nice but she didn't care.

"Not really. Not my thing."

He knew, though, it was her thing. She was a good dancer. He'd watched her from the balcony at one of the last events. Dancing, laughing, having all sorts of fun with a couple of trolls who were surprisingly light on their feet. He noticed quite a few of the other guys there were watching her, too. He was good at a lot of things but dancing wasn't one of them and neither was making a fool out of himself on purpose. Especially in front of her.

"I'm sure you'll find all sort of guys just dying to be asked by you. See ya." And with that he had left, calling for his dog, Mango, who was busy further down the beach chasing seagulls.

After that, she never really talked to him much, even though he seemed to come out and support almost every event she competed in. In all of her time at St. Annalise, she had been asked out plenty of times, but he was the only guy she had cared enough to ask out. And the only one she still watched even when she didn't really want to.

Chapter 9

What To Do Next?

Location: St. Annalise Island

Six years had quickly passed at St. Annalise and graduation was looming. For Sandra and Cappie the years there had been close to idyllic. Sandra had stayed busy with classes, island activities, and whiling away time with her friends, and Cappie had found work helping a fellow boat dweller, Thomas Jackson, restore antique boats. She and Thomas had developed a friendship that seemed finally to be just on the verge of developing into a full-blown romance.

True to the promises in the school brochure that had brought them to St. Annalise in the first place, Sandra was set to graduate with a wide variety of skills and knowledge on many topics. The school offered a post graduation year as an option, and Sandra, after talking it over – and over – with Cappie, had almost decided she would stay for that.

"I could go to a university in the United States, Cappie. That might be exciting since I've never been there before," she said, thinking out loud again about her choices. "I see stacks of college brochures in the library from there all the time."

Cappie wanted to support whatever her charge wanted to do next but felt like the extra year at St. Annalise would be in Sandra's best interest. "There are still several topics you want to study, not to mention you don't really know what you want to do next. Staying here would give you extra time to make a plan. Plus, Spence and Birdie will be here, too."

Cappie was right. Sandra really had no idea what she wanted to do next. She wished that some kind of direction would arrive in a bottle like the last time she had to make a really big life-changing decision. She started checking around the boat every day, just in case, but there was never anything except Rio looking for an extra rub on her tail fin. Well, except once when there had been an old tin canister that she got excited about. When she pried open the lid, though, the only thing inside was a piece of sea kelp and a really mad crab that had somehow managed to get itself trapped.

She knew she would be happy staying at St. Annalise but a restlessness seemed to be growing in her. Sometimes she thought she might like to sail to somewhere cold next since she and Cappie had lived in the tropics for so long. Just to change things up. Then she would change her mind and decide it would be better to head back to where her parents disappeared. For a while even, she was thinking about going somewhere inland and living away from the sea for something totally different.

Nothing seemed to interest her enough to take any action until the day the letter arrived and everything became crystal clear.

Chapter Ten

The Letter That Changes Everything

Location: St. Annalise Island

"So any idea what this assembly's about?" Sandra asked Spencer as they walked into the main hall and took seats next to each other.

"None. Nobody seems to know."

Sandra looked around. The hall was buzzing with chatter but quieter than usual for so many people. "You're right. Everyone looks as puzzled as we do. I think this is only the third time we've been called together for an announcement assembly the whole time we've been here."

Spencer shrugged his shoulders. "Beats me. Maybe it's another storm warning, like the first time. Hope not since that turned out to be a bunch of worrying for nothing."

"We were lucky, Spence," Sandra said.

The other time an announcement assembly was called it was to let them know that one of their favorite professors was missing at sea (which had brought back a flood of memories for Sandra.) Since both prior occasions had been for solemn announcements, the students were understandably on edge this afternoon.

"Where's Birdie?" Sandra asked Spence, watching the stage as Christina Annalise moved to the podium.

"Right here," Birdie said as she slid into the seat that Sandra had saved next to her. "Look at the headmistress. She's smiling."

"Good afternoon, good afternoon, students," the headmistress repeated as the group grew quiet. "First, let me say that unlike our prior assemblies, today is about something very positive. In fact, I am so excited that I am going to get right to it!

"Before I do, though, I have to apologize to our younger students. This opportunity is only for those students who are sixteen human years of age or older – or will be by December 25 of this year."

Even though they didn't yet know what they were missing out on, there was a low rumble of disappointment from the younger students that echoed throughout the hall, interrupting the headmistress. She had the complete attention, however, of all the older students.

"I know. I understand that some of you may be disappointed. I called you all together nonetheless, because this news will affect you - all children everywhere really." Christina Annalise cleared her throat and smiled at the group. "This is an unexpected turn of events, perhaps one of the most significant in modern world history." Now she really had every student's attention. Even Jason was in the big hall listening.

"Guess it's not a storm," Spence leaned over to the girls and said.

"Shhhhhhh!" they both snapped at him in return.

Christina Annalise was holding a piece of paper high in the air. "This letter arrived this morning by North Pole Express."

Now the whole hall was full of chatter. Sandra glared around her, trying to stare everyone into being quiet so she could hear this exciting news.

The headmistress gave it a moment and then spoke louder into the podium's microphone. "The letter is addressed to all of us here at St. Annalise Academy from an elf named Zinga who is apparently an assistant to Santa, as in THE Santa Claus. Rather than paraphrase what it says, I'd like to read the letter to you."

With a big breath and a quick smile, she began.

Dear Believer of Christmas Magic,

Santa sends his greetings to you and his hope that you or someone you know will be interested in this unique opportunity that I write of today!

Perhaps you heard the news from Santa's recent press conference that our world population is quickly reaching a point exceeding the ability for our Santa to serve in one night. Even his magic has limits of time.

I am sure you agree that we simply cannot have children left out! So, Santa and the North Pole Claus Council have determined the time has come to add a second Santa.

Yes, a second Santa! We know this is a very new idea for everyone, but we believe it is the perfect solution to this grave situation. And such an exciting opportunity!

Have you ever dreamed of being Santa? Do you love children? Have you got a jolly laugh and merry twinkle in your eye?

Letters are now being accepted and must be delivered by regular post no later than one week from this letter's date. Simply state what your qualifications are and why you should be considered. Applicants will be selected based on qualifications, sincerity and a little bit of magical luck.

Santa himself will select the individuals chosen as finalists who will then compete for the position in a challenging competition at the North Pole.

We know there are so many who would be very good, but we need just one who will be extraordinary. Good luck to you!

Merry Christmas!

Zinga

Zinga
Elf Extraordinaire
Director, World Outreach

When Christina had finished reading she asked the group, "Does anyone have any questions?" Hands went up around the hall, and the headmistress spent the next thirty minutes answering questions – mostly with "I don't know" as her answer. Finally, the announcement assembly let out, and as the students left the hall, each of the eligible students was handed a copy of the letter addressed specifically to him or her. Sandra, Birdie and Spencer all received one.

"Can you even believe it?" said Sandra as soon as they were outside, reading their own copies of the same letter. "We could be Santa!"

"First of all, you're not a guy and you're not the right size," said Spencer. "And even if you were, why would you want to be Santa?" Nothing about the opportunity appealed to him at all. He was certain he wasn't that interested in cold climates or big adventures particularly. He liked science and spending time in the lab. There were plenty of thrills for him to be found right there.

"I think I'm with Spence on this one, Sandra," said Birdie. "I mean it would be fun and all for, like a day, but it's a ton of work. Plus it's really cold there and the whole world is counting on you. That seems like too much responsibility to me."

"What? How can you even say that, Birdie? Are you really telling me you're not going to apply?"

Her two friends just looked at her until Spence sputtered out, "So I take it that means you're going to? I never really thought of you as the Santa type," he paused and grinned. "But now that I do, well, I think you'd be a good one."

"You'd be a great one, Sandra," Birdie told her friend sincerely.

Sandra felt like they were right. Somehow, she just knew she could be a good Santa, maybe even a great one. "Well, get ready, because I'm applying and I'm going to get it!" With that, she said she'd see them later at the beach and took off running to share the news with Cappie.

Chapter 11

Cappie's Support

Location: St. Annalise Island

"Cappie! Cappie! Look at this!" Sandra was hollering, as she ran up the dock and hopped onto the *Mistletoe*, letter high in hand. "It's a letter from the North Pole saying they are looking for a second Santa. I could be Santa, Cappie. Listen. 'Ho, Ho, Ho!'" Only Sandra's "Ho Ho's" sounded a lot more like "Oh, Oh, Oh!" especially since she was trying to catch her breath from running full speed to the *Mistletoe*. They both burst out laughing.

"What on earth are you talking about, Cassandra?" Cappie said, using Sandra's full name and looking stern despite the laugh, largely because Sandra had given her such a scare running down to the boat hollering that way. So Sandra spilled out the whole story from the morning and read the letter out loud to Cappie – twice.

"And, Cappie, I almost forgot, you got a letter too! You can apply too. Maybe we both could be the second Santa. We could be Santa Two and Santa Three!" Sandra grinned as she handed Cappie's letter to her.

"Oh, ho ho yourself, Sandra! Now you're really talking crazy talk. I haven't got the energy and I already know the best Santa they could possibly select is standing right in front of me. You, my darling, would be an excellent Santa," Cappie said, cupping Sandra's cheeks in her hands. Whatever her young charge wanted, Cappie wanted for her – even this. Sandra smiled back at her, appreciating again how lucky she was to have Cappie and all the love she gave her. Then a frown crossed her face.

"Cappie, do you think I'm too young?" she said looking fully worried.

"You meet the age requirement so I don't think that would be a problem."

"Do you think they'll think I'm too skinny?" she said as she turned her slender figure side to side, trying to puff it up a bit.

Cappie stifled a smile. "Thankfully, you are much thinner than Santa, but I think they would welcome a young, fit, energetic Santa. Really, Sandra, think about all that you are, not what you aren't."

In reality, Cappie did have some doubts. Sandra *was* young and slender. Not to mention, a *girl* with no work experience to mention at all. Still, Cappie sincerely believed Sandra could do anything, including being Santa if she wanted.

"Let's look at what day it is due," Cappie said, as she walked to the calendar pinned to an outside wall and checked. "You have just under a week to send your reply. Sleep on it tonight and you can start on your reply tomorrow if you still want to apply."

"I don't need to sleep on it, Cappie. I already know."

In Sandra's mind, she was already busy crafting her response. She slapped on her headphones, cranked up some calypso music and headed to the bow's deck where she always went to think. This was the most important thing she felt she had ever written in her life, and she needed to concentrate. At last, as clear as a sunny island day, she knew she had found what she wanted to do.

CHAPTER 12

Sandra's Response

Location: St. Annalise Island

Oh Oh Ohhhhhhh! Sandra stared at the notebook on her lap, more frustrated than she had ever been. She wanted to express why becoming the second Santa was so important to her, but she had no idea what she really wanted to say.

She had been at it for hours, with wadded up pieces of paper strewn around the deck from where she had thrown them, and she still couldn't settle on what to write. She wanted Santa to know what was in her heart but she always had a problem sharing how she really felt. Except to her parents and Cappie. For some reason, the advice one of the counselors had given her when she was trying to decide what she wanted to do after she graduated from St. Annalise came back to her.

"Life can seem complicated and overwhelming at times and sometimes it is. You will be asked to respond to difficult situations and may struggle trying to decide what to do when faced with different choices. The mistake most of us make is to over-think things and pursue complicated solutions.

Instead, listen to your heart. Follow your passions. Keep your next steps simple and true, and life will flow easier for you."

At the time, she had felt like that was nice but not all that helpful, but now it suddenly offered her inspiration and clarity. With that in mind, she began again.

Why I Would Like to be the New Second Santa

by Cassandra Penelope Clausmonetsiamlydelaterra...

This is the hardest letter I have ever written because it's so important, and I'm not sure what to write really. My guardian, Cappie, says I have some unique abilities that I can offer you. For instance, I speak seven current languages, four lost languages and know about six additional dialects from countries around the world. I am willing to learn more.

I am excellent at gymnastics and acrobatics, and those skills would surely be helpful in gift delivery. I also enjoy tai chi and karate.

I earned top grades in my geography classes and can tell you the name of almost every country and major city on a map. My geography teacher, Professor Countryman, said I was the best student he's ever had in class. (I hope that's not bragging to tell you that.) I even know the exact loca-

tion of the lost city of Atlantis, although no one currently lives there, especially not any kids.

I have taken physics and quantum physics and actually liked them much more than I thought I would. It made sense! I suspect that Santa uses some of the laws of quantum physics to accomplish all that he does in such a short time.

I have lived many places and would have no problem moving to the North Pole. I have recently been thinking, in fact, that after living in the tropics for most my life, I would enjoy a colder climate for a change.

I know I'm young and, you know, skinny compared to Santa. And okay, I don't have any experience at all being a Santa. But I believe part of being Santa must be about knowing in your heart that you would be right for it.

I am sure you will get lots of applications but I would love, love, **LOVE** *to be considered!!! It's* **SO** *important to me. Even if I'm not, though, I will keep all the magic of Christmas in my heart and promise to support the second Santa whoever he, or she, is. J You will be able to count on me for that.*

Merry Christmas!

Sandra P. Clausmonetsiamlydelaterra...

P.S. Please say "Ho Ho Ho" to Santa for me and thank him again for all the perfect gifts he has brought me every year. I remember seeing him when I hid behind the tree one year.
P.P.S. I have been practicing my "Ho Ho Ho's!"

Sandra watched Cappie read the letter for the fifth or sixth time. Sandra kept making small, minute changes, and Cappie would have to read it all over again. "What do you think?" she asked Cappie for the fifteenth time at least.

"It sounds perfect to me, Sandra. What matters, though, is that you like it. Have you said everything you want to say?"

"I think I have, Cappie. I tried to write from my heart and I think I'm happy with it."

"Then let's send it off today so you're sure not to miss the deadline."

With that, Sandra popped it into a big white envelope and addressed it in her favorite sparkly red ink. *Please*, she thought as she sealed it, *please Santa, pick me.*

Chapter 13

The Finalists Are Selected

Location: the North Pole

From the minute the Population Alarm had gone off at the Pole, the place had been put into elf chaos. First of all, their oversized ears were still ringing from how loud the clanging had been. Secondly, and most importantly, elves like simple routine. They like knowing their job and supporting Santa to help children everywhere. This whole business of two Santa's had caused great concern, and the Claus Council had been called together for another emergency meeting.

It was the council that had decided what had to be done after the alarm went off. Besides Santa, the group included:

Zinga, his ever-present assistant
Toasty, exceptional at organization
Wicket, responsible for real estate and construction
Breezy, skilled at weather monitoring
Tack, director of research & development
Rumpus, overall director of toy production
LuLu, director of marketing

Violet, director of product design

Violet loved everything purple, but was named for her pretty color. She was a rare elf indeed. Not tan or green like most, but a very pretty shade of purple.

This was the group also charged with organizing the letters pouring in to be the new second Santa, and that was the reason they were meeting on this North Pole afternoon, barely a week after Santa's press conference.

Like she predicted in her application letter, Sandra wasn't the only one interested in the popular position. Within just a couple days, so many applications began to arrive that the elves had to clear out a big corner of one of the toy warehouses. After reading them, the elves placed the letters in one of three piles:

No

Yes

Maybe

The No pile had thousands of applications piled high. Most applications, in fact, ended up there. Though it was hard to explain, it wasn't just whether you had the qualifications or not to be Santa. All elves have the ability to sense whether someone has Pole-related magic in them (most people don't and even those who do usually don't know it.) Only those applicants with it could be moved to the Yes pile. As a result, the Yes pile was very small, smaller than any of them had anticipated. The Maybe pile hadn't really been used. Well, sort of, but the one application in the Maybe pile didn't quite seem like it belonged in the Yes or the No pile so that's why the elves had reluctantly made a Maybe pile. They felt like maybe they should have a Maybe pile and maybe they shouldn't. They still hadn't quite decided.

Most of the applicants were surprisingly young – between eighteen and thirty in human years on average – although there was one that was only seven, a little boy from London who wrote earnestly about why he thought they should lower their age limit. Santa asked the elves to set that one aside in case they ever needed a third Santa in the future.

Processing the applications turned out to be more challenging than any of them had anticipated because there were so many that brought the elves to tears. As happy as they are generally portrayed, the truth is, elves cry easily. They cry over sad stories and they cry over happy stories, and there were lots of both from the applicants wanting to be the next Santa.

"This is going to be harder than I thought," Santa said to Zinga, speaking loudly to be heard over the crying elves, as they strolled through the warehouse full of the piles of applications. Zinga handed out tissues as they went along. "There are so many applying but so few in the Yes pile."

Santa was right. It was wonderful that there were still so many Santa Believers out there and so many that were interested in being Santa. It was worrisome, though, how few had the necessary qualifications and magic combination. Many of those that could fully qualify hadn't even applied. They understood that, while it was a wonderful opportunity, it was also far more than just a job. Sure, it came with generous perks like a free home, worldwide travel, secure employment, a long life, adoring children, and loyal employees, but it also would be a dramatic life-change for whoever was selected. Most people weren't ready for that big of a leap. In the end, nearly 103,000 applications were received and from those only five made it into the Yes pile. Just five.

"Five!" Santa boomed as he was seated at the table and the Claus Council emergency meeting was called to order. He felt caught off guard by the small number but kept in mind that they just needed one. "Well then, Toasty, please step up and tell us something about each one."

"It will be my pleasure, Santa," said the elf who had got his name because he preferred toast with cinnamon and sugar for breakfast rather than the more common, always popular, oversized cinnamon rolls with extra thick frosting that most elves loved.

"Let me start with our very own Rollo Kringle. Rollo, as you know, is one of the head elves here at the North Pole. He is a master-level toy maker and one of the few elves who applied. Personally, I think he will be hard to beat."

"Yes, yes, excellent choice," Santa said, nodding his head at the selection. "Rollo has always been interested in learning more about the delivery side of this business and this could certainly be his chance. Who's next, Toasty?"

"Next on our list is Klondike Tannenbaum, who hails from Germany and is also part elf. He looks a lot like you, Santa," Toasty added as he handed a portrait photo to Santa from the applicant. "Klondike writes that he is an exceptional tree decorator and has won several national titles in his native country."

"Ho Ho Ho!" laughed Santa. "Yes, I see the resemblance in this picture. I have to say, the last time I saw Klondike had to be about fifty years ago. He's added a few pounds since then. Doesn't look a day older, though. Ho Ho Ho!"

Toasty continued with his report. "That brings me to Redson O'Brien, who prefers to go simply by 'Red.' Mr. O'Brien, er, that is Red, is part leprechaun, a banker by trade and very thin, sir. Perhaps that's the wrong look for a second Santa."

"Now, now, not necessarily, though I do find it difficult to understand how he stays that slim since I happen to know his wife is an outstanding baker. Why, she made me a chocolate cheesecake once that I still remember to this day. It was almost as good as something from Mrs. Claus. It had this crispy chocolate crust, with an oozing, creamy chocolate center and this crackly choco-"

"Sir!" Toasty interrupted, afraid Santa was drifting off to one of his favorite topics – talking at length about desserts. "Sir, we really should push on with the whole list."

"Quite right, Toasty, quite right. Redson O'Brien is also an excellent choice for a finalist."

"Thank you, Santa. Our next finalist's name is Gunther W. Holiday IV. Gunther is our youngest candidate. He, too, is part elf, loves children and comes from a large family of twelve children. He's the second to the youngest and an accomplished athlete."

"I know of Gunther, in fact, I know all of the Holiday children," Santa said. "As I remember he goes by Gunny, and the family lives on one of those huge state-of-Texas-size ranches in the state of Texas." He looked around smiling, and the elves all broke into giggling over his Texas joke. Santa's silly jokes were their very favorite. "That ranch of theirs is so big that, the first time I visited, I arrived at the front gate and then had a hard time finding the house! Ho Ho Ho! I'm glad he applied and made the list. We have one more?"

"Yes, our last finalist is Nicholas Navidad from, well, several countries in South America actually, so let's just say from

South America. Nicholas is a world-renowned child psychologist. Perhaps some of you remember reading his piece on *Setting Christmas Expectations for Your Child* in the October issue of *Family Holidays* magazine." To that, Santa nodded his head in agreement but none of the elves. They all liked reading comic books and pretty much nothing else.

Santa, however, remembered the write-up well. "Nick Navidad is known for his insights into children's creativity," he said to the group. "Additionally, as I recall, he is fluent in at least six different languages including a dialect almost no one knows, spoken by an Amazon jungle tribe. And he certainly has the right name for the job. He's another excellent choice."

"Thank you, Santa," Toasty said as he handed Santa the file on all the finalists. Zinga slipped out of the meeting to get busy sending letters out to the finalists – and to all the applicants who hadn't been selected.

"This is a fine list of candidates," Santa muttered as he worked his way through the pile, spending a few moments with each before he looked up to address the gathering of elves all waiting for the final acceptance. "Thank you. I know this represents a lot of work by all of you to select these five finalists. I'm puzzled, though, and wondering, did we get any applications from women? Did we only receive applications from men?"

There was a momentary awkward pause as some of the elves shuffled about in their seats. Elves never like Santa to be displeased and they hate awkward moments. Lulu and Wicket reached for the huge candy bowl in the middle of the table, and each of them ate seven Foaming Fizzers in quick succession. Violet looked blue and Rumpus started mindlessly swaying back and forth, while Breezy blew air into a huge gum bubble. It popped loudly and finally Toasty cleared his throat and looked miserably at his records. "Well, yes, we did receive some, Santa. Less than a thousand actually, which was a surprise, and only one really met the full qualifications. Then we decided she was too young, and, well, sir, she's a girl." He said the last part fast, understanding now that Santa wouldn't mind that she was a girl. He finished quickly with, "So we put her in the Maybe pile." He handed Santa the very thin file and sat down flustered.

"Ah, Cassandra Penelope Clausmonetsiamlydelaterra..." Santa read when he opened the folder. "I knew her grandfather and have followed her story through mutual friends. Yes, indeed. I'm so glad she applied." Santa said this last part more to himself than to the whole group while he looked over her letter. "Do any of you know anything about Cassandra?" Santa finally asked. Everyone shook their head "no."

"I rather thought not or it's very likely she would have made your Yes pile rather than the Maybe pile. Well, then, since she has applied, and I think she deserves our consideration," Santa looked around the room, "now's a good time for me to share some of her story with you."

Chapter 14

Selection News

Location: St. Annalise Island

A letter from the North Pole addressed to Christina Annalise arrived at the island just hours after the Claus Council had met and decided on their five finalists. In addition to Sandra, three other students from St. Annalise had applied for the second Santa position, and the headmistress called them all to her office to share the news from the Pole.

She was so excited she couldn't stand the suspense. While she waited for the students, she opened and read the letter. The news wasn't what any of them were hoping for. "I'm so sorry to have to tell you that no one from St. Annalise was selected as a Santa finalist," she told them regretfully as soon as all four were there. She knew they were disappointed, but she was very proud of them for applying. She kept the meeting short since there was little more to say. "I know that any of you would have made a very fine second Santa," she told the small group. A couple of them shrugged but none of them said anything in response. As they shuffled out, the headmistress held Sandra back. She had seen a tear run down her cheek before Sandra wiped it away, and Christina wanted to be sure the generally cheery student was okay with the news. "Sandra, I know you were especially excited about this. You would have made an exceptional second Santa."

"I'm okay, Christina," she said, brushing off another tear and feeling more disappointed than she had expected. "I didn't really think I'd make it anyways, I guess. I mean, I was hoping, but I knew there would be a lot of competition. I could have done it, though."

She was already heading out of the office, not wanting to talk to Christina about it anymore. She knew Cappie was waiting on the *Mistletoe* for the news but she headed the opposite direction. She wasn't ready to talk to anyone.

Chapter 15

Cassandra's Story

Location: the North Pole

For elves, the room was unusually quiet, while everyone waited for Santa to begin. Elves love a good story and this tale about Cassandra sounded like it might be one of the best they had heard in several days.

"So the story of Cassandra begins, as many of the best ones do, with her parents Cassiopola 'Cassy' and Sanderson 'Sandy' Claus falling in love, getting married and having their lovely daughter.

"Several years ago – at least six, maybe more now – Sandra's parents were lost at sea. I'm not sure if anyone knows exactly what happened. At the time of the disappearance, the family and their boat captain and close friend, Captain Margaret Richmond, were moored in a bay off one of the islands of the South Pacific where they were homeschooling Sandra and focusing on a method of teaching that lets you learn many languages simultaneously. As I recall, Sandra can speak multiple languages with ease." Santa paused, turning to Zinga. "You know, we really should look into bringing that program to our school here," he said.

"Excellent idea. I'll look into that, sir," said his efficient assistant.

"Good, good. Now where were we?" Santa paused in thought. "Ah yes, in the South Pacific. Sandra was on shore that day, and Captain Richmond, 'Cappie' to Sandra and her parents, had accompanied her. Sandy and Cassy apparently were spending their days in pursuit of testing the affects of world pollution on the local environment. Cassy was an accomplished artist and anthropologist, and Sandy was a talented musician and environmental scientist." Santa smiled, recalling the happy couple he had met. "They studied the world and ways to help make it better. It's what they loved most beside Sandra."

"On that day in late summer, it is widely believed that they had set out on the *Mistletoe* for a cove off one of the neighboring islands to photograph unusual coral they had heard of through one of the local islanders. At least that is the plan they had shared with Sandra and the Captain. The mystery then is why the boat was found in an area about six miles from the cove, in calm seas, and most puzzling and devastating of all, without any sign of its occupants."

Santa stopped to pass around the big box of Christmas-patterned hankies to the now crying elves. He knew this would happen and was prepared.

"Despite weeks of searching, Sandy and Cassy were never found." Now the little group of elves melted into wailing, and even Santa had to pause to gather himself.

"Now, now, hard things happen to families all over the world," he said, trying to comfort the group but only making them wail louder thinking about tragedy befalling so many. He spoke up louder in hopes of helping them move to more positive thoughts. "All of you know that, sadly, just because you are born a Claus doesn't mean you necessarily stay a Santa believer and believe in the magic of Christmas," he said while the elves nodded their heads and dabbed at their eyes in agreement. "No, indeed, under these kind of circumstances, it seems many people lose their heart and faith and often quit believing in many good things – including themselves, sometimes in the power of love, even in Christmas magic.

"Not Sandra, though, in spite of her despair and her deep loss. Her belief in goodness, in light, in joy, in the work of Santa Claus and what all of you do here, and the magic of Christmas barely even wavered. She and Cappie celebrated that Christmas after the loss of her parents with sadness but with joy as well. I still remember seeing her on the *Mistletoe* that night, tucked in asleep behind their tree with a picture of her parents next to her, waiting for me."

With that, he sat down, opened Cassandra's file again and looked around the room. "Can I see a show of hands of everyone willing to add Cassandra P. Claus... to our list of finalists?" Elf hands went up around the room.

Like she had done earlier after the finalist list was presented, Zinga raced out the door. *Always so efficient*, Santa thought. This time, that had proved to be too true.

Chapter 16

Not So Fast

Location: St. Annalise Island

As she left Christina's office, head down, trying to hold back a flood of tears and take in the disappointing news, Sandra ran smack into Jason and lost her balance. *Just my luck*, she thought, *of all the people I'd have to run into right now, it had to be him.* As he steadied her, she noticed he was looking at her with curiosity, but there was something else in his stormy gray eyes, too. She thought, with surprise, that it might be concern, but she decided that couldn't be it and the idea passed quickly.

"I didn't make the Santa list," she blurted out not really knowing why she was telling him of all people.

"Oh is that all?" Jason said looking relieved by what she told him, which annoyed her completely. She felt distressed and dejected and had dared to hope that he might be just a little sympathetic.

"Is that all?" Sandra responded too strongly, feeling vulnerable and emotional. She stepped back from him, now angry.

"I'm sure you thought that I never had a chance but it was really important to me."

Jason wanted to tell her how stupid he thought they were for not picking her. He really did but instead he found himself saying, "Only guys can be Santa, Sandra."

"Oh Jason Annalise, just once, just one time, I wish –"

"Sandra! Sandra!" Christine Annalise was shouting her name. "You made it!" She was running from her office with something in her hand, and Sandra wasn't sure that she had understood her right.

"What did she just say?" Sandra said to Jason, not quite believing what she thought she had just heard.

The headmistress caught up with the pair, out of breath and excited. "You made it, Sandra! You made the Santa finalist list! A rapid fairy delivery service just arrived, straight from the North Pole, correcting the earlier letter. There was a mistake. You're in!"

"I'm in?" She said looking completely shocked with joy. "I'm in! Jason, I'm in!" She grabbed onto the boy she had liked and disliked for so long and hugged him. She hugged him big. And he surprised her by hugging her back. It was quick but it was great. Really great.

Then he ruined it.

"Why do you want to put yourself through all that, Sandra?" he groused at her. "You know they're going to end up picking some chubby old guy with a beard."

As quickly as it had begun, the moment was over. He was just unsupportive, mean-spirited Jason again. Before Sandra could say anything, Christina spoke up. "Jason, Sandra would make a great Santa," she scolded her son. "A whole new kind of Santa. Santa Claus is wonderful just the way he is, but that doesn't mean the second Santa has to be just like him." Then she turned to Sandra. "Now go share your big news with Cappie and Birdie and Spence and everyone else on the island before I do!"

Sandra looked from Christina to Jason and again seemed to catch him off-guard. He was looking intently at her with some kind of expression on his face. *Was that pride? Frustration? Affection, even?* The questions flew through her head as they always seemed to when he was around. She just could not understand him at all. *And really why should she care what he thinks anyways?* she thought to herself. She knew people who would be excited for her and tell her so. Off she ran!

CHAPTER 17

It's Official

Location: St. Annalise Island

"Cappie! Cappie!" Sandra screamed as she raced down the dock to the *Mistletoe*. Cappie was instantly alert, her heart pounding, wondering what was wrong that would cause her charge to be running and screaming in such a loud way. Then she saw her huge smile and the piece of paper she was waving around. *Could it be that Sandra had actually made the finals?* she thought. Cappie hardly dared to hope since it seemed like such a radical idea. But still, the way she was screaming –

"I made it! Cappie, I made it!" I made the second Santa finals!!!" Sandra's screaming brought Squawk flying over from a few boats down where he had been working on sweet-talking one of the younger students into handing over his gingerbread cookie without much luck. Sandra was always his top priority. The cookie could wait. Sandra handed the letter to Cappie who read it quickly but carefully.

Dear Cassandra Claus . . .

Greetings from the North Pole and congratulations! The selection committee was very impressed with your sincere essay and your unique qualifications. I am completely pleased to tell you on this fine, beautiful day that you have been selected as one of our six finalists to compete for the new position of second Santa.

We are sure you can understand that it is imperative that we find the perfect candidate to fill this important role. As such, all six candidates will be given full access to the North Pole during our High Christmas Season so you can fully appreciate the magnitude of the job. Additionally, while you are here, you will be interviewed and participate in a series of physical and mental exercises all designed to identify the best individual for this position.

There is no time to waste! In three days time, we will send a Reindeer Express coach to transport you and one other person of your choice (providing they, too, have North Pole clearance, of course.) Please plan to be away from your home for approximately one to three weeks.

Congratulations again on this honor! Over a hundred thousand applied but only six were selected. We sincerely appreciate your interest in this important position, and I personally look forward to greeting you in just three days time.

Giggles and hugs,

Zinga

Zinga
Elf Extraordinaire
Director, World Outreach
P.S. Please forgive me for the earlier confusion over not being selected. The Claus Council here experienced a delay before settling on its final candidate list.

"squawk! Sandra did it!" squawk!" the bird said getting in on the fun.

Well I'll be darned, thought Cappie. *She really, truly made the cut*. Happily, sometimes, dreams do come true, and Sandra was going to get a shot at one of hers.

She turned to Sandra who was watching her expectantly, a smile on her face big enough to be seen at the North Pole. At that moment, Cappie would always remember thinking two things: that Sandra had never looked more beautiful or more like her mother; and that her parents, like Cappie, would be so proud of their talented, gracious, vivacious daughter. Thinking of it all brought Cappie to tears – something very unlike her.

"Cappie, what is it?" Sandra said, the smile gone and concern for her beloved guardian taking its place.

"I'm just so proud of you," Cappie said, laughing a little through her tears. "And I know your parents would be too." Now Sandra was crying, too, and for an instant they both stood there, tears flowing, enjoying a moment of complete joy and complete sadness missing the two people they had loved so much.

After a moment, Cappie pulled herself together and started thinking practically again on all they would need to do before their Reindeer Express showed up. In just three days! There was a lot that would need to be done before they could simply be gone for three weeks. As Cappie ran through the long chore list in her head, she realized they needed to get right to packing. Sandra could start by finding their suitcases from somewhere in the dusty storage area of the *Mistletoe* and –

"Sandra! Sandra!" The suitcases would have to wait as the two heard yelling coming from Birdie and Spence who were running down the dock at full speed. "Is it true?" Birdie blurted out when she came to a full screeching stop, so fast that Spence nearly ran into her.

"I'm sorry, is what true?" Sandra asked coyly.

"Christina said you got a letter from the Pole," Spencer said sounding a little puzzled and winded.

"Yes, it's true!" Sandra said, hopping up and down, simply unable to contain her excitement a minute longer. The girls started hugging and screaming. Spencer stepped back, grinning. "No way, no way," he kept saying, shaking his head, but in a really good way, like someone stunned after hearing great, unexpected, news often does.

All four of the group sat down and read the letter over and over. Cappie made fish and fruit for dinner, and even Squawk got in on the fun by reciting his favorite part of the letter. ". . . giggles and hugs . . . giggles and hugs . . . squawk!" he would add and flap his colorful wings around. Within a couple hours, it seemed like most the island had heard the news and come by the *Mistletoe* to see if it was true and congratulate Sandra.

Truth be told, most of them were probably skeptical about Sandra's chances – Santa was a man, after all – but every one of them would be cheering her on. It was late when Birdie and Spence finally headed back to their dorm rooms.

Chapter 18

Learning What She Didn't Know

Location: St. Annalise Island

While Cappie had enjoyed every minute of the impromptu evening, there was something weighing heavy on her heart, something she had to tell Sandra. Something she knew she had to take care of that night. Somehow, every day since Sandy and Cassy had gone missing, Cappie had managed to find a reason for why it wasn't the right time to talk to her charge about it. She knew now, for sure, that she could no longer put it off. Sandra deserved to know. More importantly, she needed to know. Sandra had been tucked away, safe with few worries, on St. Annalise but that time was quickly coming to an end. She would soon be going out into the bigger world. Plus, it occurred to Cappie that Santa himself might well know Sandra's background and share it with her first if Cappie didn't. It was time for Sandra to learn what Cappie knew and she started the conversation as soon as Sandra's friends had left.

"Sandra, there's something I have wanted to talk to you about for some time and with this second Santa opportunity, it's now imperative that you know," Cappie tried to sound nonchalant even though she felt everything but that.

Sandra yawned and stretched. "What is it, Cappie?" she asked. "Is it about one of my classes? Surfing? Is it about mom and dad?"

"It's nothing about your classes or surfing but, yes, it is something about your parents." With those words, Sandra went from feeling close to exhausted to feeling fully awake.

"Your parents," Cappie began, searching for the right words to convey what she wanted to say. She started over. "We both know how wonderful your parents were, but the truth is no one has ever told you, not even me, exactly how special they were. Of course, you know that your dad was a member of the Claus family. That's special all by itself, and while not a close relative, you are, indeed, distantly related to Santa and even have a bit of elf blood in you from that side of the family."

Sandra was listening closely, wondering just what Cappie was concerned about. This was great news! While Sandra had always sort of wondered if she was related to Santa Claus in some remote way, she had never really considered that would mean she was of elf descent.

"That's cool, Cappie! Why haven't you ever told me that? Why didn't mom and dad? They always told me I was part elfin, of course, from mom, but elf, too? That rocks! Maybe I'll find out that I have an amazing natural talent for making toys."

Cappie smiled. Her charge was always so positive. "You never know, do you?"

Many people get elves and elfins confused but the two are actually quite different – at least in height. Elves are generally small (under four feet in height), commonly green or tan in color, with large ears as a primary feature. Besides having extraordinary hearing, they adore children and make outstanding toymakers. Additionally, they live very long lives. Surprisingly, while they are capable of magic, they generally prefer living simple, dedicated lives in service to children. Almost all "100% elf" elves live at the North Pole where they are most comfortable. Centuries ago elves and humans lived and mixed more regularly together, and, as a result, many families have elf ancestry in their family history. Most however, have no idea.

Elfins, on the other hand, are more like humans in appearance, only more stunning and less known than elves. Elfins are generally tall and lean, beautiful in appearance with very green eyes as their most outstanding feature. While they, too, tend to have extraordinary senses like enhanced hearing and sight, elfins also, generally, have magical abilities that make them sought out by some and hunted by others. Consequently, those with the strongest powers tend to work to blend in with the rest of the world as much as possible. (That is not always the case, however. Some elfins have little magic except to exude a strong magnetism and have often used that ability to excel on stage and screen. Many of the most popular Hollywood movie stars, throughout the ages, have actually been of elfin descent.)

"Well, there is more to the story," Cappie continued. "While your father was a descendant of the Claus family, your mother, as you know, was elfin. What you don't know is that she was a Leezle," Cappie paused before pushing on.

"Many centuries ago, when elfins lived openly with humans, the Leezle family was the royal ruling family. In the fifteenth century, between war and famine and disease and, I am sad to say, outright killings by humans and other species who envied their special powers, the elfins were largely killed off or captured." Cappie shuddered. "The Leezle family was believed to have died off at that time and have no direct descendants. But that wasn't completely true. It was a story put out by a consortium of strong protectors to keep the few remaining members of the family alive. A sister and a brother had survived, and powerful elfins hid them away to keep them safe. Your mother was a descendant of that sister, which means you are a descendant as well."

Sandra was staring at Cappie, not sure she was fully understanding or believing what she was hearing. What a day this had been! First, she had made the list to be second Santa and now she was finding out she was elfin royalty. *Does it get any better than this?* she thought and smiled to herself. Still when you got right down to it, she felt it really didn't make sense. She liked the idea but, c'mon, royalty?

"Cappie, are you sure? I don't feel like a 'princess' of any sort. Nobody ever bows to me." That idea made her laugh out loud. "I can't fly, disappear, read minds or do any kind of magic at all. Mom never seemed like she could either. I do have great eyesight and I can read really fast. And I remember stuff – but so do most my friends." This last part she seemed to be pondering out loud to herself.

"This is important, Sandra," Cappie said to her firmly. "It's who you are. Your parents didn't want you to know when you were younger, or the world to know for that matter, because there are still individuals out there who would likely choose to harm you. I worry that that is what happened to your parents that day."

As soon as she said that, Sandra's mood and attention to the matter changed completely. "Cappie, do you think someone hurt mom and dad because they found out mom was a Leezle? Why didn't they hurt me, too?"

"I really don't think that's what happened?" Cappie said soothingly, trying to sound convincing on something she wasn't sure about at all. "Honestly, I think they had a tragic accident. But it's likely there are people and creatures out there that probably would have harmed your mother if they could have."

Sandra considered that for a minute not wanting to believe it could be true. She still was not convinced she could possibly have any kind of royal background. Birdie did, of course, on her mother's side, and not only looked the part of an African princess but also had her special ability to talk with birds, thanks to the magic from her father's side. That made total sense to Sandra.

"Cappie, I really have never felt special in any way. Okay, yes, I do have the green eyes and extra long eyelashes, which I like, but really the only special thing about me, as mom would say, is my hair and –" she stopped mid-sentence and a look of understanding crossed her face. At that moment, she knew without a doubt that Cappie was right. She was royalty. *How totally amazing*, she thought as she sat back hard in her chair.

"My hair. My hair sparkles because I'm a Leezle, doesn't it?"

Sandra's hair was not like anybody else's that she had ever seen – except for her mother's. Her red hair didn't just shine, it sparkled like it had been sprinkled with crystal clear glitter. She didn't really have any hair until she was about four years old, which was unusual, but her mother never seemed overly concerned. When it finally started to grow, it was magnificent – thick, wavy and a deep red color that her mother had called "Christmas red." It grew long fast and . . . sparkled! Her mother taught her how to mix up a special shampoo to use that gave her hair a glistening shine but kept it from sparkling. "But I like my sparkly hair," little Sandra had protested. "I love your sparkly hair, too, Cassandra," her sweet, patient mother had replied. "But we must keep it a secret just for us because other people would be terribly jealous if they knew we had such pretty hair," and she tickled her little girl until she rolled all around in a fit of giggles. Sandra loved the memory and had accepted that her mother knew best. Cappie had mixed it up and Sandra had always used the special shampoo, without question, knowing it was a small connection to her mother and what she had wanted her to do.

"It is," Cappie nodded. "That's why it's so different and so beautiful and why Cassy had to be sure you learned to hide it even though she hated so much not being able to let you show it. To anyone who was looking to harm you, your hair would be a sure sign of your heritage. No one outside the royal Leezle family has ever been born with that wonderful glittering red hair. It is said it was a gift from a royal leprechaun family to the Leezles centuries ago, in repayment for a Leezle having assisted them when they were in great danger."

Sandra had no response. She couldn't think of a single thing to say. There were so many questions to be asked, but right now, at this moment, her mind was completely overloaded. All she could focus on was that she was not just an elf related to Santa Claus but also a royal elfin. Wow.

She realized that Cappie was talking to her. "Sandra? Are you all right?" Cappie was worried and looking for some kind of assurance that she had done the right thing in sharing the information and waiting till now to tell her. "Should I have told you all of this earlier?" she finally asked.

"I'm fine, Cappie. Really I am." She moved over to where Cappie sat and leaned against her like she had done a thousand times before. Cappie folded her into her arms. "I'm just trying to take it all in. It's okay that you haven't told me before. I think it was good that I didn't know, and I think it's important that I know now. Mom and Dad would have wanted me to know. Even though I don't feel special, I always knew Mom was."

"She was, baby, she was," Cappie said quietly, stroking Sandra's tired head. Then she moved her charge around so she could look directly at her. "There is more to share with you about your heritage but that can wait until after the tryouts – after the holidays. Right now, the most important thing for me to tell you is that you absolutely cannot tell anyone what I have shared with you, and I mean no one, Cassandra. Your parents kept this secret for a reason, and we must continue to guard it as well. I have shared it with you now because it really is your secret to keep."

"I understand, Cappie. I won't talk to anyone except you about it. No one. Not even Spence and Birdie. Now, though, I'm going to bed. No more surprises today!" she said tiredly as she kissed Cappie goodnight.

As she headed exhausted to her berth, she knew she wouldn't tell anyone. Just what would she say to Birdie and Spence anyway? "*Hey Birdie, hey Spence, by the way, guess what I found out last night? I'm an elfin princess?*" They were such good friends they would probably believe it all faster than she did, but, right now, she couldn't even say it with a straight face. She was tempted to tell Jason, though – and insist he bow!

Chapter 19

Next Stop – North Pole!

Location: From St. Annalise to the North Pole

The three days they thought they had to get ready turned into two. A second post had arrived, asking the two of them to be ready at midnight and asking that they not mention the time to anyone else. The hope was that the coach could arrive for pick-up without drawing a crowd. Santa preferred to keep North Pole business to a low profile whenever possible.

Sandra knew Birdie and Spence would be disappointed not seeing her off, and it took a lot of restraint not to tell them the new departure time. They already were completely bummed about not going, but it was Squawk who was being especially awful about being left behind.

"squawk . . ." he said whenever he saw Sandra. ". . . I always go. You always take me. squawk . . . "

Sandra threw up her arms in frustration. "You know I would take you if I could, but I can't, so please stop. You're driving me nuts!"

" . . .not fair, not fair," Squawk said. Then he rattled off a litany of "squawks" in Sandra's face before he flew off to the bow of the *Mistletoe* with his back to her still squawking.

On and on he went until Sandra turned away from him as well, shaking her head. She wished she could have taken him, but the instructions were firm: the finalist plus one and that meant Cappie or Squawk. In this case, that meant Cappie.

She was glad the coach was coming at night when Squawk would be sleeping. She knew he would have tried to follow them otherwise, and the cold ole Pole was really no place for her wonderful tropical friend.

As promised, the Reindeer Express Coach arrived one minute after midnight on the third day. Despite the very late arrival (or very early, depending on your point of view), Sandra and Cappie were wide awake on deck, waiting expectantly with their bags packed. Sandra was so excited she was flitting all around. Cappie couldn't help but smile as she watched her.

They were both scanning the night sky, watching for their ride, when somehow, silently – magically - it was just there. It landed on the *Mistletoe* deck with ease and room to spare.

"Ahoy there," called out the elf who was handling the reins of two large reindeer.

Even though they knew a ride was on its way, Sandra and Cappie found themselves staring dumbfounded at the tiny elf and big reindeer. Despite this shocked state, they managed to pick up their bags and move toward their "ride." The coach appeared to be a three-sided "box" made out of a lovely cherry-colored wood that sat on sleigh runners. There were two bench seats in it. The driver was sitting in the front one, and there was a door on the side of the coach that opened to the more enclosed bench area. On the other side of the coach was a large picture window. An intricate, royal-looking insignia, with the letters SC intertwined together, was carved into each side.

"Lidio!" said the little coach driver, smiling, as he hopped on to the deck. "Lidio" was an elfin word that the two both knew but didn't hear often. It roughly translated in English to "hello, hi, good day" or even "welcome."

"H-h-h-hi," Sandra managed to stammer. She thought she was ready for this adventure but she found herself now totally taken aback. *Why*, she thought, *I think I'm talking to a full-blooded elf*!

"Yes, indeed you are," said the elf.

Sandra was even more startled. Had she said that out loud? Had he read her mind? She looked over at him, not knowing what to think. Almost scared to think anything!

"No," he said. "You did not say that out loud, though it quite seemed so to me. I can often read thoughts – particularly when they are about me. Most elves have one or two special gifts – things they are really good at. Reading thoughts is one of mine.

"Navigating is my other," he added.

"Please allow me to officially introduce myself and my two reindeer assistants. I am Zoomer at your service." He stooped low and swept his top hat their way. "And these two fine fellas," he nodded at the reindeer, "are Comet and Dasher." The two reindeer now nodded in their direction, and Sandra's and Cappie's eyes opened even wider, if that was possible. "You are Cassandra and Captain Richmond, I believe?"

"I am, we are," stammered Cappie. "But please, call me Cappie."

"And I'm Sandra," Sandra managed to sputter. "It's a pleasure to meet you," She looked toward the reindeer, nodding quickly at Comet and Dasher as they did the same to her.

"I don't mean to be rude Zoomer but are you sure the two of us can fit inside this lovely coach? We're rather tall." asked Cappie.

She looked skeptically at the mode of transportation that had landed on their deck. She had good reason to be skeptical since the coach looked to be about the size of a refrigerator box – barely big enough for one of them to ride in and rather uncomfortably at that.

"Plenty of room, plenty of room," Zoomer said smiling. "I brought one of the new expandable models." He reached over, pressed a button on the coach "dashboard" and, just like that, it lifted off the deck about a foot in the air and expanded in length and width to more than double its size. "This baby has the new heated seats and foot rests," said Zoomer patting it affectionately. "And plenty of trunk space for your trunks." He laughed at his own, little joke. Cappie and Sandra just looked at him and then started to laugh, too. To Sandra, the whole experience was already fun.

"Well, ladies, we need to be off. Are you ready?" he asked as he looked at them both.

Cappie looked over at Sandra to check just one last time, but Sandra was already reaching for the door. "We definitely are, Zoomer."

"Then in you both go."

"Eeeeeee eeeeee eeeeee" came a noise from the water, just as Sandra was getting into the coach. Zoomer jumped with surprise but Sandra knew immediately what the noise was.

"Rio! Ssssshhhhh, you'll wake up Squawk," she said to her dolphin friend. "Thank you for coming to say goodbye," she whispered to the dolphin as she reached down to give her a quick scratch over the side of the boat. "Remember that I love you. And tell Squawk that again, too, for me. Keep him company while we're gone, okay? He's going to be lonesome and mad. We'll see you soon."

She stood up and said to Zoomer, "Okay I'm really ready. Bye, Rio." The dolphin eeeee'd her goodbye and Sandra climbed in. Only seconds after she sat down next to Cappie in the most comfortable seat she had ever sat in, Zoomer tugged lightly on the reins and the sleigh lifted away with a swoosh.

"Look, Cappie!" said Sandra pointing out the window. "Look how little the *Mistletoe* is already!" Before they could even sit back in their seats, the *Mistletoe* and St. Annalise were completely out of sight.

Sandra began to laugh with glee. "It feels like we're flying,"

"Because we are!" Cappie said.

"Please sit back and enjoy your ride. Our full travel time will be several hours," Zoomer said. "Perhaps you would like to use that time to watch one of our many Christmas movies. Or you might want to get some sleep because once we get to the Pole, you are going to be very busy. Very busy, indeed."

The whole idea of sleep seemed impossible to Sandra. She wanted to savor everything about the experience. Nonetheless, within minutes she drifted off and was sleeping soundly. Not Cappie, though. She was wide awake for most of the ride, cradling Sandra and wondering what she had encouraged her cherished charge to get into.

Chapter 20

First View of the Village

Location: the North Pole

"North Pole!" Zoomer called out as they started to circle above a picturesque village.

"Sandra, we're here," Cappie said, lightly shaking her still sleeping charge.

"Cappie!" Sandra said as soon as she realized where they were. "You let me sleep? What all have I missed?"

"Hours of nothing until just this minute."

Sandra looked out the coach window with anticipation as Zoomer circled them once more around before landing softly. Everywhere she looked, everything was more then she imagined. There was so much to take in. Right away she noticed that everything sparkled like a first snow does in moonlight. She could hear Christmas songs in the distance and could see a small elf playing an assortment of instruments with a happy elf next to him dancing away.

"That's Buddy," said Zoomer, again reading her thoughts. "He's our troubadour. If you have any favorite songs you want him to play, just ask him and he will – as long as they're Christmas carols, of course. And the dancing elf next to him is Ellen. She dances everywhere she goes because it makes her happy."

"It works on me, too," Sandra said. "I'm already happy but watching Buddy and Ellen adds even more to the fun."

The buildings were painted in bright colors and had curving rooflines. There were Christmas decorations and lights and big packages and bright trees all around the "town." And the people! The people were the best. *Well, maybe*, she thought, *you couldn't think of them all as people.* There were far more varieties than just humans walking around.

"We don't mind," said Zoomer. "Up here at the Pole, you'll meet elves, elfins and humans – even some fairies and a sprinkling of other kinds as well from time-to-time. But you can call us all people. It cuts across all different types of individuals and no one will object." He was certainly right about the mix. Outside the coach window as they landed, Sandra saw itty-bitty elves walking alongside taller elves. She also saw what looked like human men and women, and, once, a group walked by that looked like they were talking to a tall penguin! And the penguin was talking back! Wow, she thought, Birdie would have fit right in.

She rubbed her eyes, making sure she was fully awake, but they were still walking and talking – including the penguin – when she looked again. She saw three elves go by who appeared to be in a serious conversation with a couple balls of flittering lights that she assumed might be some of the fairies Zoomer had mentioned. She felt awestruck by it all –and she also felt like she had come home.

"We've landed at your hotel," Zoomer said as he opened the coach doors. "Breezy will be meeting us here to check you in and show you around." The elf then turned to Sandra and deeply bowed. "I feel honored that I was fortunate enough to act as your escort here today, Cassandra Penelope Clausmonetsiamlydelaterra... If you ever need anything at all, please call me. I am at your service. The boys," and he nodded toward the reindeer who were nodding in response, "and I, wish you all the best. We think you would make a wonderful second Santa." With that, Zoomer helped Cappie and Sandra out of the coach, and as quickly and quietly as they had arrived, Zoomer and the Reindeer Coach were gone.

They had stepped out right in front of the Arctic Circle Inn, which looked like a standard hotel in most parts of the world – when it was Christmas that is and it was decked out for the holiday. Plus, none of those hotels had toy soldiers as bellman like this one did.

Surprisingly though, the decorations and bellman weren't what caught Sandra's eye first. "Look, Cappie, at the pretty spider there," She pointed excitedly to the sidewalk area. "Who knew they had spiders at the North Pole? Oh my goodness, it could get stomped on if it stays there." Without even thinking whether it might be harmful or not, Sandra stooped down, scooped up the sparkling spider and placed it safely on the hotel wall. "You really must stay off the busy walkway," she admonished the spider as it skittered quickly away.

"Cassandra Claus! What if that had been dangerous?" Cappie exclaimed and reached over to take Sandra's hand.

"We're at the North Pole, Cappie! Of course it wasn't."

"Please take their bags to Suite 24," said a very pretty elf with long dark hair tied with a big red bow, as she walked through the doors toward them. One of the toy soldiers came forward, moving surprisingly fast in spite of his stiff gait, and was off with their luggage into the lobby and down a hall. "Everything here is magical, Cappie!" Sandra found herself exclaiming.

The lovely elf was now greeting Cappie and Sandra. "Welcome to the North Pole! It's so nice to have you here. I'm Breezy."

Sandra was charmed by the name. Right away, it made her think of the tropical breezes that would blow into St. Annalise, helping to cool the hottest days and making wind surfing the best.

"I always wanted to try that sport," Breezy said, smiling at her.

"You hear thoughts like Zoomer!"

"Yes, but he's more of a showoff about it."

Cappie and Sandy officially introduced themselves and followed Breezy into the hotel lobby. "I'm sure you have lots of questions. First, though, we thought you'd want to freshen up. If you follow me this way, I will show you to your suite." For such a little elf, she was hard to keep up with. "It's important that you know that there are only a few of us who actually know who all the candidates are. Santa has asked us to keep that news private. I'm sure it won't surprise you to hear he likes surprises." She smiled at that. "Elves won't ask, although some will surely guess, or even simply be able to read your thoughts, but please do not share directly why you are here with anyone you may meet before the announcement tomorrow morning."

"Of course not," said Sandra.

"Also," Breezy continued. "We know that the latest and greatest is all about being connected by cell phones, computers and that World Wide Web . . ." She said each word with just a hint of disdain in her voice, ". . . but none of the contestants are allowed to access any of these during your time here at the Pole. It is all part of keeping the competition fair. I'm sure you understand. That includes you as well, Captain Richmond"

"Of course, of course," the two responded in unison.

"Thank you. So here we are at your suite. Let's plan to meet back in the lobby for an early dinner in an hour. I will bid you goodbye until then." She turned and, like Zoomer, somehow was quickly gone.

The two opened the door to Suite 24 and gasped with delight. Oh, their room! It wasn't like any hotel room they had ever been in. For starters, right in the middle of it was the most beautiful Christmas tree ever. It was at least twelve feet tall, with twinkling lights and sparkling tinsel. Two four-poster beds were tucked on each side of the tree with plush red and green plaid bedspreads. The movie, *A Miracle on 34th Street,* was playing on the TV. On each bed was a stocking with their name on it, stuffed with treats like Christmas stockings usually are. There was candy, a deck of cards shaped like round ornaments, red-striped socks that looked like the pair Breezy was wearing, a tube of peppermint-flavored toothpaste and a toothbrush that looked like a candy cane that Sandra could hardly wait to use.

"Can you believe this?" Sandra asked as she spun around and around the middle of the room, taking in all the details.

"Watch out that you don't get dizzy," Cappie said, but she was laughing, too.

Sandra plopped down on her bed to get a better look at what else was in the stocking. When she did, she noticed there was a big envelope on her pillow with a note from Breezy taped to it, "*Please bring this with you to dinner – B.*"

Next to a sitting area with a couch and two rocking chairs, there were two full bathrooms complete with large dressing rooms. The two unpacked, showered, changed and were glad they were headed to dinner since they were both hungry. The room had a big bowl of fabulous-looking fruits, and each of them wolfed down a banana and some grapes. Plus, despite Cappie recommending against it so she wouldn't ruin her appetite, Sandra got into her stocking, looking for something fun to eat. She looked through all of her choices and decided on a bag of gummy candies – one of her favorite treats. She popped a few into her mouth, and, before she could even chew, the candy started "hopping" all around pushing her head up and down and side to side! They hopped back and forth, up and down, cheek to cheek, making her and Cappie laugh so hard she finally had to spit them out.

"Oh my goodness!" Sandra exclaimed.

"What on earth was that, Sandra?" asked Cappie trying hard to catch her breath from all the laughing.

Sandra grabbed the wrapper it had been in. "They're called Hopping Frogs," she read. "Caution, eat one at a time. Boy, that's for sure." And they both had to lay on their beds with a bad case of the North Pole giggles.

Finally, they gained their composure back and made their way out to the hotel lobby, where Breezy met them and recommended a diner nearby called "Eat, Drink & Make Merry." The menu featured foods from around the world. Sandra ordered a big bowl of macaroni and cheese and a large mug of cocoa. Cappie decided to try "Noodles ala Merryinera" – a local favorite that Breezy recommended. Both meals came with crusty whole grain bread and big green salads. Cappie skipped the cocoa for a cup of coffee. Even though it was dinner time, Breezy ordered a giant cinnamon roll and a big mug of hot cocoa with "extra whipped cream, please." Sandra and Cappie would later learn that in the same way whole grains and vegetables acted like fuel for human bodies, sugar did the same for elves. Not to mention, elves love any kind of sweet treat.

"So, let me tell you about what you can expect in the days ahead," said Breezy as she daintily licked a scoop of whipped cream from her finger. "First off, congratulations for being selected as one of the second Santa finalists! What an honor! Zoomer picked you both up, and other coaches have arrived with the other contestants. There are only six of you who made the finalist list so you should feel very proud."

Sandra felt neutral about it all really. She was glad to hear there were only six, but she wasn't necessarily proud about being on the list – more like relieved –and a bit anxious as well. After all, it wasn't like she was the one selected yet.

"There is one thing I wanted to mention to you," Breezy continued casually. "Frankly, it's probably not even worth bringing up, but I don't want to you to be surprised or anything like that." Oddly, now the pretty elf seemed to be having trouble looking at Sandra as she spoke and was studying the swirls in her giant cinnamon roll. "Actually this news should make you especially proud when you think about it. You see, as it happens, you are the only female contestant who made the finalist list. There are four men, one elf and you. You are also the youngest." Breezy finally looked at Sandra to measure her reaction to this news. Despite the fact that she had seen pictures of Santa hundreds of times, heard the stories, knew them all by heart in fact, for some reason it had never occurred to Sandra that she might be the only girl – or the youngest. Never. The news was more than a surprise to her.

"No other girls?" she asked Breezy, looking a bit stunned. Breezy shook her head. "I never considered that but I suppose it makes sense, doesn't it?"

"Not really," Breezy said. "We had no preconceived notions before we made our choices."

"Is it okay for the second Santa to be a girl? I mean it didn't say that girls couldn't apply."

"Of course it's okay," said Breezy. "In fact, Santa was delighted when he heard you were interested."

"He was?"

"Absolutely. I was there myself when he got the news. You should have seen the big smile on his face."

Sandra was quiet for a moment while she took it all in and then asked sincerely, "Breezy, do you think I have a chance?"

"Are you kidding? You have an excellent chance, Sandra. Never doubt that you do," Breezy smiled as if she had a secret. "The way Santa talked, I think he is especially fond of you."

Sandra's eyes lit up. "Really? I feel the same way about him, but I don't want to win unless I deserve it, of course."

"Believe me you won't. Santa will only select the best candidate, no matter what. It's too important of a job for him to play favorites." Breezy said. "Personally, I just can hardly wait for my elf friends here to meet you! There are going to be so many of us cheering you on – girls and boys – I just know it.

"So, enough on all of that for now, would you like to hear more about your schedule?" Sandra and Cappie both nodded.

"Good. Tonight is your free night," Breezy continued. "You can do whatever you like. I recommend you make it an early night, however, since the week ahead is going to be very busy.

"I'll make sure she gets enough rest," Cappie said. "Although I'm sure if it was up to her, she'd be out exploring the Pole."

"You know me pretty well," Sandra said, smiling sheepishly.

Breezy winked at Cappie. "Tomorrow the real action starts and it starts early. First thing tomorrow, you'll get to meet Santa and the other second Santa contestants along with many of us who live here at the Pole."

Sandra clapped her hands in glee. "I can't wait!"

"My suggestion to you is to remember that while this is a social event, many of the selection committee members will be there interacting with all of you and getting their first impressions," Breezy said. "You won't know who they are, but they definitely will know who you are." Breezy was charmed by the excitement on Sandra's face. She continued. "Just be yourself. Then, starting tomorrow morning after the breakfast get-together, you will be in official try-outs for the next four days. Each day, you will have a short session with the other candidates about issues related to being Santa. After the group sessions, you'll participate in competition activities. Every finalist will complete the same tasks."

"What kind of tasks will they be?" asked Sandra feeling a little bit anxious now. She hadn't really thought about what all would be involved in getting selected to be the new Santa.

"You'll get the full list at tomorrow morning's breakfast," answered Breezy. She could see how apprehensive Sandra looked and tried to calm her nerves by touching her hand. "I am sure you are going to do excellent. Otherwise you would never have been selected as a finalist.

"There is more information about the week ahead in this packet," she patted the envelope Sandra had brought with her. "You'll also find a map of the North Pole area and a list of fun things to see and do while you're here. I don't think you will have much time to do many this visit. This evening is your best chance to take advantage of your free time."

"I'm going to check out what looks like the most fun to do," Sandra said.

"Speaking of fun things, there's one thing I can tell you about that all of us here at the Pole are looking forward to so much! The last evening you are here, there's a big dance called the Claus Christmas Cotillion being held for the announcement of the second Santa. Did you bring your ball gowns like it suggested in the information we sent?"

They both nodded yes. They had actually made their own. Cappie had a lovely blue velvet dress, and Sandra was excited about the emerald green satin number she had made in her costume class but never had had a chance to wear.

"For everybody here at the Pole, the dance is the highlight of the whole week. I'm going with Rumpus, the manager of toy assembly," Breezy added smiling shyly. "Okay, any questions?" She slurped down the rest of her second big cup of cocoa as Sandra and Cappie hesitantly shook their heads. Of course, they had questions! Probably a million of them but none came to mind at that minute. "Well, good, that means that we're done for right now. You two can get settled and ready for tomorrow," she said scooting out of the long booth seat.

"I'm genuinely pleased to be assigned as your escort while you are here at the Pole, Sandra. Captain, it is also a pleasure to serve you. You will have quite a bit of free time each day while Sandra is in her competitions. I'll check in with you each morning on what you would like to do that day."

As they left the diner, Sandra smiled at their waiter again, "Thank you for the great service," she said warmly. "Please tell the chef our dinner was excellent. We ate every bite!"

"I'll be on my way now and will see you tomorrow morning in Happiness Hall," Breezy said. "It's just across the way in the middle of the toy factory building. Lindigo." With that, she waved and skipped off in the merry way that they would learn all elves do.

"Lindigo," they both responded in unison. It was elfin for "enjoy a deep sleep" and Sandra had heard it only from Cappie since her parents were lost.

"Let's go explore the village, Cappie," Sandra suggested excitedly as soon as Breezy was gone.

Cappie had not slept at all in the Reindeer Coach on the trip to the Pole and was now exhausted. "Sandra, let's head back to our room for a short nap first and then we'll get out and explore for awhile."

"But Cappie," Sandra started to protest and then realized how tired Cappie looked. "Okay," she finished.

They headed back to their suite. Cappie kicked off her shoes and lay down on her big bed. In no time, like Sandra on the Reindeer Coach ride, she was not just resting but completely asleep. Sandra tiptoed to the door and let herself out. She had no interest in napping when there was a Pole to be explored!

Chapter 21

Exploring!

Location: The North Pole

Sandra suspected Cappie wouldn't be happy about her striking out on her own, but since Cappie was sure to be asleep for at least an hour, it gave her a chance to get a good look at the local area and still be back before Cappie woke up.

From the air as they landed, Sandra had seen that the village was in the shape of a big circle so she knew she couldn't get too lost. The toy factory with its enormous picture windows and four main entrances was in the center of the circle. The windows made it possible to see some of what was going on inside. The map showed one entrance right across from the hotel, one entrance on the opposite side across from Santa's house, one close to elf housing and the last one across from the city park.

Sandra headed to a store next to the hotel full of unusual hats that she had spotted earlier on their walk to the diner. Unfortunately, they had gotten to the Pole after most the shops had closed so she could only window shop. Next door to the hat shop was a store full of every kind of snow boots you could possibly imagine. Sandra set her sights on a pair that was temperature controlled so they could be heated on the coldest days and cooled when you were inside or as the day warmed up. In store after store, the windows were full of unique delights. There was a book store with nothing but Christmas books, a card shop, a fabric store with only Christmas-design fabrics and even a clothing store full of nothing but very short clothes. She passed seven candy stores, several cocoa shops and the post office, which reminded her she needed to get a postcard off to Spence and Birdie first thing tomorrow with a p.s. to Squawk. After strolling past them all, she decided her favorite store was a funky old shop that featured ancient elfin history books and maps of the world – "topside and underworld."

On the other side of the post office was something Sandra had never seen but always wanted to – a UFO parked at the Pole! It was a shiny silver color that glowed. Twinkling lights flitted around it. There was a "front door" to the grounded spaceship with a small sign next to it. Sandra, too curious to stay away, approached the door cautiously. The sign read "Universal Fairy Organization" and she burst out laughing. UFOs were fairy transports! That explained a lot. She could hardly wait to tell Spence and Birdie about it.

Eventually she made her way to the village park where she stopped for a few minutes at the entrance area and listened to Buddy play his two guitars, harmonica and even a ukulele. The little troubadour was so small that he actually rode on top of a large golden retriever as he played. The scene made her smile. *He's really good*, she thought as she wandered on. The troubadour called out "thank you," and Sandra was glad she only had happy thoughts about the elves.

While the shopping area had been quiet, the park was busy with activity. She was on a walkway across a snowy field away from the busiest area. Across the way, she could see families picnicking in a covered, heated picnic area and children building snowmen, riding sleds and building forts. It seemed like a perfect, fun-filled place to be Sandra was thinking when she was suddenly, painfully, brought out of that reverie. "Ow!" she said loudly reaching for her head and whirling around. Something had hit her on the back of the head – hard – and that was even with her thick hat on.

"Ow!" she exclaimed again rubbing her head. She looked around to see what or who had caused her jolt of pain but there was nobody there – or even anywhere close-by. When she looked down, she realized she'd been hit by a snowball. *Probably some naughty child*, she thought to herself, already forgiving them as she reached out to pick-up the snowball and toss it toward the open field. It was strangely heavy for a snowball she realized as she picked it up – because it was no ordinary "snowball." Instead, it was a perfectly round white rock with the words "Go away" scribbled on it in big black letters!

Chapter 22

Pole Pong!

Location: The North Pole

For an instant, Sandra was taken aback. Surely no one wanted her to go away. This was the North Pole where happy things happened. She scanned the park area again looking closely in all directions to see if she could spot where the guilty culprit who had thrown the rock was hiding. Nothing seemed amiss. *Well*, she finally thought, *obviously naughty children lived all around the world – including at the North Pole.* She decided to put the matter aside, tucked the rock into her pocket and set out across the park to the building with a flashing sign on top that read "Santadome." A bump on the head wasn't going to keep her from making the most of her trip around the Pole.

Out in front of the building was a flashing reader board: **Elves with Attitude Coming January 7!!!** * **Hockey Playoffs: Pole Prowlers meet the Northern Blights December 17** * **Play Pole Pong Here** * Even from across the street, Sandra could hear the noise of people cheering.

At the door she was stopped, "Viewing or playing?" the attendant asked. "Just viewing, I guess," Sandra replied and the attendant let her in.

She was surprised to find how much the inside looked like a sports and entertainment dome that could be in any city around the world. There was gray concrete everywhere – none of the bright colors that you found around the rest of the village. There were posters of coming events lining the wall and two concession stands near the door she came in with a long line of chattering elves waiting. As soon as they saw her, the chattering stopped all at once and the group stood gaping at her as she walked by. She felt awkward but gave them a little wave and smiled shyly at each. She smelled caramel corn and cocoa and chocolate chip cookies. There was loud cheering and applauding coming from the main arena, and she made her way to the seating area where she hoped to watch part of the hockey game.

Except it wasn't hockey that was being played. It was Pole Pong! The arena area was like no sports center Sandra had ever been to before. The dome rose much higher than she had realized from the outside. She had entered the arena area at about half way up. The side she entered on was floor-to-ceiling seating like most sports domes everywhere. But in place of seating on the other half of the arena across from her was…a giant pinball game! That's what it looked like to Sandra anyway. The game play area – the "board" she would learn it was called – was set at a steep angle, like a ski slope really, with big posts positioned down the sloped playing area. Each post had numbers printed on them "20, 10, 5, and -10."

At the top of the board, lined up in slots, were four elves – two on each team – sitting in large inner tubes. Way down at the bottom of the board was one more player for each team. Those players – the "paddlers" – each controlled three big paddles, all located at the bottom. The paddles could move 180 degrees from left to right and right to left and there were spaces in between them about three feet across. As Sandra found an empty seat, a loud buzzer went off. Two players, one from each team, dropped in their inner tubes down the board and a wild game of Pole Pong began! It took Sandra a little while to catch on, but basically, from what she could tell, the goal of the game was to get as many points as possible by hitting the posts placed around the playing field – like a ball in a pinball game – and by hitting the other player's tube. Making the game truly crazy and especially fun was that the posts acted like springs when they were hit and would send the players flying in any direction. Sometimes they would bounce off other posts, sometimes into the other player and sometimes straight toward the bottom. Plus, there were two round dots on the board that were lit up and kept changing color. If either player ran over them when the color was bright red, the inner tube would suddenly deflate, the player would slide down the board to the bottom and was out of the game.

Players lost points by hitting any minus-ten post or by illegally using their hands outside of the inner tube. They made their way around the board by using a middle wheel inside the inner tube that let them steer a little bit and by flinging their weight from side to side. Plus they had help from their paddlers below. As a player, called a "ponger," got close to the bottom, he would try to hurl his inner tube toward one of the paddles so his paddler could use it to send him high up on the board again and he could "pong" around for more points. The longer a player could pong around the board the more points he was likely to score. When he missed one of the paddles or had a deflated tube and hit the bottom of the board a loud bell would ring and he was done. "Pong!" the referee would shout and the crowd would cheer and boo. The next ponger from up above would then begin his wild ride down the board (there were teams for women as well, and co-ed, but on this night just the men were playing.) The players would continue to "drop and pong" until one team hit 300 points and the final score would flash on the reader board. Winner! It was fast! It was wild! And it looked like a lot of fun.

The little elves were lightweight and would fling around the big pong board at breakneck speed in their inner tubes. The more aggressive players would try to bounce their opponents toward the bottom while trying to get as many points for themselves at the same time. Gravity would eventually force them all down and the paddlers raced to shoot them back up before they triggered the bottom bell.

Sandra found herself shouting and cheering with the rest of the crowd and had lost track of time watching the unusual game. She had also found herself watching the paddler for one of the teams and he had caught her doing it. The thing was, he wasn't an elf. All of the other players on both teams, including the other team's paddler, were clearly elves. But this paddler looked human. In fact, to Sandra, he looked like quite a cute human. He was good at the game, but despite his size advantage, he was not quite as good as the small, skilled elf playing paddler for the other team. That seemed to definitely frustrate him – especially when the other team outscored his three times in a row. A couple times he hollered at his own pongers, and, once, he had stomped over to the referee, pointing at the other team about something at the end of the round. After he walked off, the referee awarded the other team five extra points as some kind of penalty against his team, so it seemed like his feedback hadn't been well received. Sandra knew she was too big to be a ponger, but she could hardly wait to have enough time to learn how to be a paddler.

"Sandra! SANDRA!" hearing her own name being hollered startled her out of her focus on the game and the human paddler, and she turned to see a concerned Cappie headed down the stairs to where she sat. "Sandra, what in the world were you thinking?" Cappie asked. Sandra had hardly ever seen her look so angry with her. "You left the room without letting me know? You didn't think I'd be worried? You could have left a note."

"I just couldn't sleep, Cappie. I knew you wouldn't like it if I went out exploring by myself, but I planned to get back before you woke up so you wouldn't worry."

"I think you've done enough exploring for one evening." Cappie's voice was still stern but softening now that she knew Sandra was safe. "It's after eleven o'clock Sandra."

She had been gone four hours! She could barely believe it. It helped her understand why Cappie was upset. She looked once more at the paddler she had been watching and noticed that he was looking at her, too. But he should have been watching his ponger.

"Pong!" the referee shouted as the cute paddler's ponger dropped to the bottom of the board and the bell went off. Bummer, thought Sandra as she smiled smugly, following Cappie out of the arena.

Chapter 23

Day One – Gunther and the rest

Location: the North Pole

"...you better watch out, you better not cry, you better not pout, I'm telling you why ..."

Sandra reached over to hit the snooze button on her radio alarm. Six a.m. Being at the North Pole, competing for one of the biggest jobs in the world, might have made sleeping difficult for someone else, but the cheery Christmas tune had brought Sandra out of a sound night's sleep. She sat up and finished the song the alarm had started with her own original twist, ". . . cause Second Santa is coming to town!" She looked over at Cappie who smiled at her with sleepy eyes.

Today the competition officially began, but that wasn't as exciting to her as meeting Santa! The big guy. The main man. The real thing. Meeting Santa, in person, was one of the things Sandra had been looking forward to the most, and she hopped out of bed, casting any leftover sleepiness aside.

She had brought a variety of colorful, comfortable clothes to wear each day and decided she would start the week off wearing a pair of green pants and a green turtleneck sweater that showed off her eyes. She wore her long red hair tied back in a single ponytail. The green outfit and her red hair made her look merry but not too "Christmassy" – perfect for the first day, she thought, before a wave of angst flushed through her.

"Let's go, Cappie," she said to her guardian impatiently. "I can't be late, no matter what."

"It's 6:30, Sandra, and we don't have to be there until 7:00," Cappie said with as much patience as she could muster.

"We don't even know where we're going for sure."

"Sandra, Happiness Hall is right across the street. How hard could that possibly be to find?"

But Cappie understood Sandra's impatience this morning. They hurried out to the lobby of the hotel where they found that Breezy was already waiting to walk to the breakfast meeting with them.

Happiness Hall wasn't like most of the places Sandra had seen so far at the Pole. The room wasn't done in the traditional set of Christmas reds and greens. Instead, it was completely painted in the happiest shade of yellow Sandra had ever seen. There was no other way to describe the color than "happy yellow." A balcony ran around three sides of the hall. At the front wall, over the podium, were clocks, showing dates and times from around the world. A giant clock in the middle was counting down to Christmas Eve.

Most people were already there. Sandra was quickly learning that although elves might be little, they all loved to eat. Breezy helped them wind their way through the crowded room and got them to their table where they were happy to recognize

Zoomer. He introduced them to the other elves sharing their table who seemed curious about them but refrained from asking any questions. A breakfast platter of pastries, sweet cereals, muffins and giant-size cinnamon rolls, of course, was served to each of them with steaming cups of cocoa. Cappie and Sandra looked at their plates and laughed at the same time. That was a whole bunch of sweet food for breakfast!

"Do you think it would be possible for us to get some oatmeal or yogurt?" Sandra asked their helpful waiter who looked like he might cry when he returned with seven flavors of yogurt to choose from but no oatmeal.

"Chef said he wished he had oatmeal for you but there just isn't any," he muttered to Sandra.

"Oh please don't worry," said Sandra sincerely to the sniffling elf, feeling bad she had made the request. "You did great. Cappie and I love all these flavors of yogurt that you brought us. Thank you very much." The little waiter stood up straighter and smiled at them both before hurrying off to the kitchen.

"If you're eating just yogurt, Captain Richmond, could I have your cinnamon roll?" Zoomer asked.

"Of course," said Cappie moving it over. "But only if you remember to call me Cappie."

"Ay Ay, Cappie," he said through a mouth already full of cinnamon roll.

"Would you mind if I had yours, Sandra?" Breezy asked before one of the other elves at the table could.

"Sure," said Sandra. She was happy to share since she was really too excited to eat anything but a few bites of one of the yogurts. Rather than eating she was spending most of her time trying to figure out who the other candidates might be in the packed room.

As soon as the breakfast plates were cleared away, an elf named Jester walked across the stage and stood at the shorter of two podiums on stage.

"Welcome, everyone, to the biggest week this Pole has ever seen." The hall broke out in applause. "Let's keep those hands together and join me in welcoming this morning, the elf without equal, the guy with a big belly and bigger heart, our man of the season... Mr. Saaaaannnnttaaaa Claaaaaauussssss..." Now the applause was thundering and everyone in the room rose to their feet.

"Ho Ho Ho! Ho Ho Ho!" Santa's voiced boomed without a microphone as he entered the hall. "What a wonderful morning," he said as he arrived on stage and walked to the taller podium. "How often do I get to see Happiness Hall packed full of elves and have Santa Believers here as our guests as well? In my hundreds of years, this is surely a first. Ho Ho Ho!"

"We have so many things to cover this morning. Where oh where should we begin? Would you like to talk about the weather?" He asked impishly. "Nooooo!" screamed the happy elves playing along.

"No?" repeated Santa. "Would you like to talk about how the stock market is doing this week? Things have been down lately –"

"Noooooooooooo!" the room of elves screamed again. Santa was clearly enjoying himself teasing the group.

"No again? Well then, let me see," he said as he shuffled some papers in front of him. He looked up from the pile, leaned forward on the podium and said conversationally to the gathered group, "Would you like to meet our second Santa contestants?"

"YESSSSS!" they thundered in response.

"Well then, why didn't you just say so?" he grinned at the room, laughing so much his shaking belly rocked the podium stand. Every elf in the room loved it. When the boss was happy, they were happy.

"Let's get right to what everyone is most excited about and meet all of our second Santa contestants," Santa said. "Contestants, as I call your name, please join me here on the front podium.

"So, first, in no particular order, from Germany, please welcome, Klondike Tannenbaum!" Santa boomed. A wild and woolly looking fella stood up in the back of the room and started to the front in big strides. He waved to the crowd as they shouted with excitement.

"Wow," said Sandra and Cappie in unison. "He looks just like Santa," Sandra whispered. Elves all around them were saying the same thing and there was a general sense that this was the kind of candidate they were hoping for. Santa was off to a good start.

"Next up, representing Ireland and the whole of the British Isles, Redson O'Brien!" This contestant was dressed all in bright green, complete with top hat, and danced a bit of a jig as he greeted Santa, then bowed to the crowd who loved it.

"He's part leprechaun," Breezy whispered to Sandra and Cappie.

"Join me now in welcoming, from the southern part of our continent and the countries of South America, Nicholas

Navidad!" A more formal individual, dressed in a stylish plaid suit seated at one of the middle tables, stood and calmly walked to the podium with some stiff waves to the crowd.

"This next individual needs very little introduction. From the North Pole, our own, Rollo Kringle!" The crowd gasped before they all stood on their feet and broke into thunderous applause that seemed to echo everywhere around the cavernous room. One of their own had made the list! As they looked around the hall for him, a sturdy-looking elf suddenly appeared via a rope swing off one of the side balconies, performed a very nice double flip above the stage and landed right next to Santa. Some of the elves in the room had to cover their ears from the loud cheering and applause that followed that entrance.

"Rollo's the local favorite, of course," whispered Breezy again when the noise died down. "Santa talked to all of us on the Claus Council though about making sure we voted fairly and didn't play favorites."

"And now, from St. Annalise Island . . .

Oh my goodness, thought Sandra, as Cappie squeezed her hand under the table.

". . . Cassandra Penelope Clausmonetsiamlydelaterra…!"

As Santa finished, and Sandra stood at her table near the back, for just the briefest moment, nobody except Cappie and Breezy clapped – the room just stared with their mouths open as if they were going to cheer and forgot how. Cappie and Breezy jumped up and began clapping even harder and the rest of the room quickly recovered and joined in. The whole way to the podium Sandra could hear the buzz. "She's a girl. She's a girl? She's a girl!"

On stage, at the podium, Santa looked her directly in the eye as if giving her some of his strength, shook her hand and whispered to her, "It's a special pleasure to have you here, Cassandra. It's a new idea to them but they'll get used to it."

"Thank you Santa," she replied sincerely. "I believe I might be the luckiest girl in the world right now." She gave him the biggest smile she had ever given anyone, nodded to the other candidates who seemed to be gaping at her as she joined them in the line-up and then turned and smiled happily to the crowd as well.

Her mind was still processing the response to her selection, so she watched, more than listened to, Santa as he announced the last candidate.

"And last, but never least," she realized Santa was saying. "Our final candidate, from the United States of America, Gunther W. Holiday the fourth!" Sandra tried to see who he was from the stage, but two of the others on stage stepped forward to see better, too, and blocked most her view. As the finalist bounded up on the stage, waving to the elves in the hall and motioning for them to clap even louder, she finally got a glimpse and realized who he was. "It's you!" she said as she found herself standing next to the paddler from last night's Pole Pong game.

"Gunny Holiday at your service Miss Very-Long-Name," he said with a Texas twang as he bowed deeply to her. The elves all loved it and clapped even more when he turned and winked at them. "I'm very much looking forward to competing with you."

After Santa finished greeting Gunny, he turned to the crowd. "Everyone, please join me again in welcoming our six candidates competing to be our – the world's – Second Santa." Santa led the loud applause as the crowd was on their feet shouting and cheering.

Sandra felt great. She thought, for a moment, *this must be how it feels to be an astronaut just back from space or a movie star who just won an academy award.* She glanced down the row of candidates and noticed that all six of them were wearing gigantic smiles.

"Now, as much as I hate to turn to heavy topics on such a merry day, I must share with you some important information this morning. It is of the utmost importance to me that everyone here understands the gravity of the issue we are facing."

With these words from Santa, the whole hall fell into a hush. "Our world population is growing faster than we anticipated. If we are not successful here this week in finding a suitable individual to serve as a second Santa, then we are going to face thousands of disappointed children at Christmas. I know none of us want that." All the elves shook their heads no, and the happy faces that were just there, were gone with many of them wiping away tears.

"I also know – and understand – that for some of you, accepting a second Santa is not easy. . . " Sandra could hear elves saying out loud, "No, it isn't Santa, it really isn't." Santa hurriedly continued, ". . . but it should be.

"These six people," he continued sweeping his hand toward the candidates, "are willing to change their lives to be in service to the world's children. Each one of these individuals is at least my equal, and it's my honor to have them here at the North

Pole with us today." He led another round of applause for the candidates.

"I'd also like to share with you that I don't like the title 'Second Santa.' The person ultimately selected, as you all know, faces a challenging position. He, or she," he added glancing at Sandra, "will be tackling the same issues as we all currently face every year in getting ready for the magical night that is Christmas Eve. To call the position 'Second Santa' would be a disservice. It would make them sound like less than me.

"Wicket here has come up with a solution for that," Santa continued, nodding at the beaming elf seated at a table near the stage. "His solution will also help resolve the logistics issues of trying to fit two Santa's here at the North Pole village. We've been at full capacity on space for some time, and I don't believe there is any way we can increase our toy production with the factory limitations we have. But, as it turns out, we happen to have plenty of space at . . ." Santa paused dramatically for affect, ". . . the South Pole and that's our plan. From this point on, our second Santa will be known as South Pole Santa!"

Even the candidates looked a little stunned as they took in this surprise announcement. The elves though were clearly crazy about the idea. "South Pole Santa! South Pole Santa!" they were chanting. Wicket loved it.

"Alright then, what a great time this has been, wouldn't you say?" Santa clearly loved working the crowd as they all cheered him on.

"So that's it for this morning. I appreciate all of your support but now it's time for us to get to work. We've lots to do. I will see you all back here in just five days for the Claus

Christmas Cotillion where we will announce our South Pole Santa selection." With that, Santa gave a final wave to the hall, sent out a final loud "Ho Ho Ho!" shook each candidates hand warmly and left the podium.

"So you think you've got a shot?" someone was saying to Sandra. It was the cute paddler.

"I'm sorry?" she replied, not really understanding what he was asking.

"At second Santa – South Pole Santa. You think ya really gotta shot?"

"Well, yes," she said a little too defensively. "Obviously Santa thinks so too, or I wouldn't have made the finalists . . ."

"C'mon, you're a girl," he interrupted her. "Whoever heard of a girl being Santa?"

Well, he may be cute, thought Sandra, *but he was clearly not all that bright.*

"Whoever heard of a South Pole Santa?" was Sandra's restrained response. "Things change." And with that she turned away and zipped off to find Cappie and get ready for the factory tour.

CHAPTER 24

Tours and Tropical Storms

Location: St. Annalise Island

While Sandra had been busy having a big adventure at the Pole, things weren't so joyful for everyone at her island home on St. Annalise.

First of all, there was one really grumpy parrot and two very bummed out friends.

"No goodbye," said Spence several times. "No way."

"Spence, what if she gets selected?" Birdie lamented out loud, looking for reassurance.

"C'mon how could a girl be Santa? I mean I love her and all – as a friend," he rolled his eyes as Birdie looked at him with a teasing grin, "and I think she can do almost anything. But Santa? She's too skinny and she's a girl. I really don't think she'll like the cold either."

". . . squawk . . . hate the cold . . . too cold . . . squawk"

Second, Jason was missing. He hadn't joined them at the impromptu celebration party the island had held the night before Sandra and Cappie left. Thomas Jackson had seen him sailing away from the island with Mango that afternoon but no one had seen him since.

And third, most significantly, a tropical storm was headed right for St. Annalise. Fast. Nobody, including Christina Annalise, who had grown up on the island, had ever experienced anything but a big rain storm before. In fact, the general belief was that the island was under an ancient protection spell that helped keep it storm-free and danger-free. As a result, no one was exactly sure what to think. Would this storm veer off like others? It seemed like it was getting awfully close. In fact, it seemed that being storm-free and danger-free was about to change at St. Annalise.

Chapter 25

A Big Dip

Location: The North Pole

Sandra shivered.

"Where did that come from?" Cappie asked noticing. "Are you warm enough Sandra?"

"I am, Cappie. I don't know what that was. Just a strange shiver. I think I shook it off," she said, bouncing up and down a bit to get rid of the unsettling feeling that had come over her.

Sandra and Cappie were blissfully unaware of any trouble back home. The contestants had spent several hours taking a wide variety of written exams that Sandra felt she had done well on. After a short break, the whole group, and their escorts, was in the process of touring the toy factory where Sandra was trying hard to pay close attention to every detail. Things like the number of toys made, the different kinds, the places they would be delivered – there was so much to know!

The tour had started in the Research and Development Center where they got to try a new candy called a Giggler because the flavor made you laugh out loud, no matter what mood you were in. Through large glass windows, they had watched a test of a new toy in development called "Tornado in a Bag." It blew the jacket right off the elf doing the demonstration! Sandra had never been anywhere that had so much creativity and technical genius gathered in one room. She decided that Spence and Birdie should be working somewhere like this. Spence was always figuring out how to do the impossible and Birdie was one of the most creative, inventive people Sandra had ever met. She would be sure and mention both of them to Santa.

The next department they toured was full of fabrics and every toy imaginable that was made from fabrics. Stuffed animals lined the walls by the tens of thousands. Another room they passed through had elves gathered around big tables playing all the newest games. In the "Mobile Toys & Gadgets" department, they were handed hard hats and warned to keep an eye out in all directions. The group stayed on guard as things went flying, sliding, walking and shooting by! Sandra's favorite room so far, though, looked like a big gym where they were testing all kinds of high-flying balls and sports equipment, including some awesome-looking skate boards. Even if she didn't get selected as South Pole Santa, at least she would know what to ask for this year. She had her eye on a bright red one with splotches of neon colors that reminded her of Squawk.

They moved from the production and testing areas to warehouses packed full of supplies. That was where it started to sink in for Sandra that there was more to being Santa than she had completely considered when she sent in her application. She'd been thinking about the fun on Christmas Eve, riding through the sky, delivering gifts, all the happy children. Being South Pole Santa, though, would be a job. A giant job. Sandra found herself feeling a little bit overwhelmed by it all.

"Is there anywhere I could get some water by chance?" she asked the enthusiastic elf who was giving them their very thorough tour.

"Just go through those doors there behind you, and you'll see a water fountain along the wall," the elf whose name was Chipper said. "The rest of us will be putting our attention right over here to. . ."

"Cappie, please take notes on anything important for me. I'll be right back."

"...one of the most exciting parts of the factory..." she heard Chipper say as she pushed through the partially opened door he had pointed out. Every part of the factory was exciting to her. She wondered if the other candidates were feeling the same way.

The water fountain was right where Chipper said it would be. Sandra found herself on a balcony that ran around another immense room. Looking around, she noticed a flickering light on the balcony wall and a sign reading "Authorized Elves Only" but, besides the water fountain, pretty much nothing else. She was the only person in the cavernous room, which brought her a nice minute of quiet after all the hubbub. After taking a long drink of icy-cold glacier water, she stepped forward to the balcony rail and saw the floor below held giant vats of paint being automatically stirred by big blades. She couldn't actually see the blades but she knew they must be there from the way the paint was being moved around. She paused at the low balcony rail – clearly set for elf heights – peering over just a little cautiously. There was red and green and yellow and bluuuuuu…

Sandra suddenly found herself flying over the balcony rail and landing right in the giant vat of blue paint! She coughed her way to the surface but right away knew she was in trouble. The top of the big tank was too far up for her to reach fully, and she could feel the paint blades pulling at her feet. She was trying desperately to hang on to the edge of the vat with her fingertips and scream for help at the same time.

"Help! Help!" she yelled, sputtering out paint. "HELP!" she screamed even louder as she felt the pull of the blades below.

"Sandra? Sandra?" she could hear Cappie's voice. "Sandra, where are you?"

"Help, Cappie! Help! I'm down here!"

Cappie took one look over the rail and screamed louder than she ever had in her life. Elves and contestants alike all came running. Chipper took one look and, well, he fainted. (Elves simply don't do well under stress.) Rollo Kringle knew where the power switch to the vats was and headed down the hall. Redson O'Brien started down a ladder located off the far end of the balcony. Somehow, though, Gunny got to her first. He had figured out how to get to the paint room floor and made his way over to the vat.

"Hang in there Long Name, I'm going to get you right on out of there," he said to her, as he pulled a table from along the wall to the side of the paint vat and climbed up on it.

Despite his calm voice, Sandra wasn't sure he'd get there in time. Her fingers were sliding as the blades tugged strongly below. Plus the paint was surprisingly heavy. Everything was slipping away, just as Gunny reached in and grabbed her out like a rag doll. "There now, I got ya," he said as she fell against him on the table, turning them both blue.

"You should be more careful," he said when he finally got a look at her and was sure she was okay. "You gave everyone a bad scare."

"I should be more careful?" Sandra sputtered. "Somebody pushed me in!"

"Sure they did. We're at the North Pole, the happiest place on earth north of Disneyland; in Santa's toy factory no less. Who here is going to push you in?"

She knew what she knew but as Cappie and the others came to help, she said nothing. The whole way back to the hotel, though, she thought about how her day had gone from being very rosy to being really, really blue.

Chapter 26

Day 2 – So Much to Do

Location: The North Pole

It was a new day and after a good night of sleep, reason had returned and Sandra decided that Gunny was probably right. She must have fallen into the paint. As he said, who at the North Pole would want to push her into a giant vat of paint? Not to mention, no one else had been in the room. She needed to pull herself together and leave that bit of unpleasantness behind. She smiled at herself in the mirror as she touched the pretty locket from her mother that she always wore, giving it a quick close look. She could have sworn it glowed when she was flailing in the paint but it looked the same now as it had always been.

"See you later Cappie," she called to her guardian who was taking a relaxing bath. Today there were no guests allowed, the contestants were completely on their own.

"Good luck, darling girl. Be careful out there," she heard Cappie call as she shut the door.

She knew exactly where she was going this morning. Her first stop was to check her exam scores that were posted in the lobby.

Day One Results

Christmas Knowledge Quiz – Top Score: Rollo Kringle

Languages Quiz – Top Score: Nicholas Navidad

Geography Quiz – Top Score: Two-way Tie: Cassandra Claus… & Gunther Holiday

Only a tie for first in geography and with Gunny of all people! She had thought she would easily take first in geography *and* languages.

"Congratulations!" she said to Rollo and Nicholas sincerely as they came away from looking at the results, but neither of them returned the greeting.

"So how's our little bluebird today?" Gunny teased as he fell in step with her.

When they reached the reindeer barn, Sandra turned to him. "I'm feeling very sunny this morning, thank you. Congratulations to you for tying with me on the geography quiz. That was one I thought I'd easily be high scorer on so I'm impressed."

"So am I," said Gunny. "I expected to have that one hands down. But then, that's what I expect for all the results." He grinned at her as they entered the barn.

Today's activities began with reindeer care and flying lessons. After a frustrating couple of hours, Sandra decided she wasn't that crazy about reindeers. No matter what she tried, she couldn't get them to cooperate into a smooth lift-off or landing. Dasher and Comet, the two she had met earlier, were the most friendly and cooperative, but none of the others seemed to want to go out of their way to make the lesson easier. Some of the other candidates had the same problems as she did but not Gunny, of course. He was a natural at it. He had a way of talking to the reindeer that they all seemed to like. When the lesson ended, Sandra decided she'd use any free time she had later to come back and work with the reindeer some more.

In between the morning lesson and the afternoon competitions, Sandra had stopped for lunch with Cappie. The two had discovered they both loved the hot cocoa served at a stand in the village called "*Liquid BonBons*" that boasted about winning "*First place in seven Cocoa Slurpoffs.*" They sat at an outside table with an outdoor heater, sipping their steaming hot cocoas and enjoying bowls of hot chili for lunch. Nearby, Buddy was playing some of their favorite carols on his guitar, and they could see Ellen down the street, dancing away, making people smile just watching her. While Sandra was busy with the competition activities, Cappie had been enjoying time in the village shops but she was preoccupied with something else as they sat enjoying the good food and the good entertainment.

"Sandra, are you sure you packed your green gown for the ball on Friday?" she asked after a while. Cappie had unpacked for both of them and was sure she hadn't seen the dress.

"I did, Cappie. It's in the blue plaid wardrobe bag. I remember putting it in the closet when we first got here."

"That's what I thought too, but it's not there now."

"How can it not be there? Of course it's there. I mean, what will I wear to the ball if it isn't, Cappie? That's the only dress I brought. I can't imagine any of these shops would have anything even close to being the right size for me."

"Well, I did see there was a fabric store. I'll look again this afternoon and if the dress isn't there, I'll start working right away on making you another. I'm sure I could borrow a sewing machine from the toy factory."

"I'm sure I packed it Cappie. Can you look again and ask at the front desk about it, too, just in case? It doesn't make sense that it'd be missing." She felt certain she hadn't left it at home but she had seemed awfully unfocused lately about some things. "Thanks for being willing to make me another if I really did forget it. I know there are lots of other things you would rather do while we're here."

With that, the two changed the topic to Sandra giving her guardian a full report on her first day scores and how the morning with the reindeer had gone. They had so much fun catching up, Sandra had to run to make the next sessions on time!

The afternoon was packed with one-on-one interviews with elves and children. By the end of the day, Sandra was getting a hoarse voice from answering so many questions. Besides the children and elves, each candidate had also spent two hours with a North Pole psychologist.

Zinga greeted the contestants in the conference room where they had all gathered, looking worn out as the long day was coming to a close. She had one last assignment for them for that day.

"You are each being given a portion of Santa's 'Naughty and Nice List,'" she said to the tired group. "Please review it carefully and mark which children were naughty and which children were nice. You can turn it into any of the elves on the Claus Council tonight or tomorrow morning." She handed long lists out to each of them.

For the other candidates, this was the simplest assignment of the competition so far. Sandra, however, agonized over the list, reading and re-reading each child's write-up. She worked well into the night, and finally, after far too many hours, she simply could not make herself mark any of them "naughty." Not one.

She turned her list into Breezy first thing the next morning with a short note on the top, "100% nice – Sandra Claus..."

As was apparently becoming his habit, Gunny fell in step with her again as she was headed to check her scores and get to the hall.

"There's nothing posted this morning, Bluebird," he said to Sandra.

"Really?" she asked, not sure if he was teasing or not. She checked the postings anyway. He wasn't teasing. There was just a note:

Day Two Results

Interviews – Elves/Children/Psychologist – All Pass

List Checking – Results not yet determined

"Told ya," Gunny grinned. "So, what's first up for us today?"

"I think we get a lesson in basic Christmas magic this morning," Sandra responded as she checked what room they were supposed to be in for that. "Then this afternoon we compete in cookie baking, tree decorating, toy assembly and wrapping. Are you any good at any of those?" She asked him smiling.

"Yep – I'm really good at all of them."

"Really good, huh?"

"Yep."

"Me too."

They both grinned, enjoying the moment of competitive camaraderie.

Chapter 27

Jason's in Trouble

Location: St. Annalise Island

No one at St. Annalise was grinning at all. Jason still wasn't home. The search boats that went out looking for him were already back because the weather had quickly turned dangerous. The heavy rain and wind had become nearly hurricane conditions. For the first time ever, the island was getting the full measure of a Caribbean storm. Christina Annalise had ordered everyone on the island – including Squawk and other pets – to the protected basement of the school where they were waiting out the storm together. Christina was beside herself with worry about her son. She wanted him home and in the basement with the rest. Not knowing where he was and if he was safe was almost more than she could stand, and she paced the floor back and forth, back and forth. Every minute the storm raged was agonizing for her.

The good news for Jason was that this was no ordinary group of people who were gathered together in the Academy's basement. This was a group with extraordinary knowledge and abilities. Every individual in that basement was busy thinking of ways to put their talents to work finding him and protecting the island.

Before they had been forced by the storm to go inside, Birdie had talked with dozens of birds to see if any of them had seen Jason. None had, but she had asked them to spread the news – and to get somewhere safe to ride out the storm.

Spence, on the other hand, was busy calculating wind velocities and direction so that some of the fairies could put at least a partial magical cloak around the island and deflect some of the worst of the winds. The gnomes were busy examining maps and marine charts to determine the most likely area Jason might be in. Traveling gnomes, of course, are natural experts at reading maps and following directions.

The usually unappreciative Jason would have welcomed the help. Just like everyone on the island, the storm had caught him off guard. He hadn't bothered to attend the celebration party the island had thrown for Sandra. He knew he'd been his usual jerk self when she shared the news about the letter with him, and he was pretty certain he was the last person she would have wanted at her party. Still sulking about it the next day, he had pushed off with Mango for a sail to think for awhile. He had a favorite little pretty island, in an archipelago of tiny islands the locals called the "Hoppers", that he called Cassandra Cay. He would have called it "some stupid little sand spit" if anyone had ever actually asked him about it but in his mind it was "Cassandra Cay."

In the little known part of the Caribbean Sea where St. Annalise was located were several groups of tiny, small and medium-sized islands that were uninhabited and, for the most part, uninhabitable. Jason's little cay was unique in that it had two distinct sides to it. On the side that Jason spent his time on, it was a flat, smooth sandy beach. On the opposite side and at both ends, the cay was rough and rocky. As far as he could tell, no one else had ever been to his small, isolated, getaway spot in the big sea.

With a good healthy breeze, it usually took a little more than an hour to get to the cay from St. Annalise. When he and Mango shoved off, there was a brisk breeze and a light covering of clouds that made for perfect sailing conditions. He lay back in the small boat day dreaming, with Mango resting against him. Apparently, they had dozed off since they were both surprised by a large wave that sloshed all over, waking them up. Mango went crazy barking as Jason, fully awake now, looked at the sea and sky with surprise and alarm. The bank of storm clouds headed towards them was like none he'd ever seen and the sea was kicking up large, completely unexpected, waves – waves far too big for his little boat. Despite his many years of sailing, he had almost no experience with storms. He could see Cassandra Cay ahead and made a quick decision that it was the best place for them to wait out this unusual weather.

Getting to the island proved to be challenging enough fighting the waves and winds the whole way, but Jason's attempt to land on the cay proved disastrous for the *Outcast*. He'd headed for the sandy side of the island where he usually beached the boat, but the waves sent them in too close to an outcropping of rocks just off the point of the sandy area. He heard the boat hit the rocks before he saw them. Before he could reach for Mango, the two were somersaulting forward with the *Outcast*, smashing against the rocks. "MANGO!" he screamed as she was washed out into the surf. The small boat lodged on top of one of the rocks for the briefest moment, but the next wave rocked it loose and knocked it fully on to the cay. Jason too was washed out of the boat into the sand and water. As he cleared his head, looking for Mango, a huge wave crashed in and began to pull his cherished boat away from the rough shore. He leaped up, grabbed the *Outcast* and pulled it with strength he didn't know he had. Somehow, he managed to haul it onto the sandy beach and away from the waves. Then he saw Mango limping slowly on the beach, struggling to take each step.

"MANGO!" he shouted, running to her against the howling wind. "Mango, don't worry, girl. Let me see, girl, let me see."

From what he could tell, her front paw had a deep cut in it. He ran back to the wrecked *Outcast* to get his first-aid kit out of the built-in chest. While he was there, he stuffed what food and bottles of water he had from a box that had been strapped into the boat, into his backpack and headed back to Mango. The wind and rain hit them with increasing force, and Jason struggled to wrap Mango's paw to stop the bleeding. She whimpered but cooperated. With that taken care of, he knew they had to find shelter.

Months ago, when he had sailed around the cay, he had noticed what looked like an entrance to a cave. The obscure entrance, as he remembered it, was above sea level. He knew it was their only chance for any protection from the storm but it meant they would have to make their way across the island.

On a calm day, it would have been a quick walk. Today, with the winds howling and having to carry wet, shivering Mango it took closer to thirty five minutes. Wind, water and sand battered them the whole way.

The other side of the cay was as rocky as the sandy side was smooth, and Jason kept slipping on the sharp rocks. He struggled to keep upright, keep hold of Mango, and find the cave entrance at the same time. Just as he thought they needed to turn back and brave it out on the wrecked *Outcast*, he spotted the entrance. With his last burst of strength, he managed to push Mango and himself through the small opening without so much as a thought to any danger that might be lurking there in the dark cave.

Chapter 28

Day Three at the Pole

Location: The North Pole

The third day of the competition reminded Sandra of sitting through one of Professor Doogle's lectures on the dangers of nuclear power. It was just too long. She had been looking forward to all of the activities scheduled for that day. They were things she felt she'd be good at. The morning's lesson on magic and the competition activities listed for that afternoon all sounded like more fun than work.

And, in fact, she had enjoyed the opportunity to learn Santa magic and was pleased with her first attempts at vertical levitating, which was used to go up chimneys. Like reindeer flying, though, she would need to keep working at it before she could really put it to much use. She managed to go in a straight line, straight up, for about four feet, which made her happy until Gunny topped her four feet by two more. Worse, he smiled at her when he did. She refused to look at him and tried hard to go further, but four feet turned out to be her best distance.

She didn't quite understand why she was so competitive with Gunny more than the others, but it was how she felt.

The superstar at levitating turned out to be Nicholas Navidad. He had gone straight up, to the top of the practice chimney, with nimbleness and ease. Meanwhile, Klondike Tannenbaum had only managed to lift off maybe a couple of inches, and even then Sandra thought it might have been just some kind of a clever hop. Red had been particularly frustrated by the exercise, as time and time again, he couldn't go up more than a couple of feet. Surprisingly, Rollo, the local favorite, had also only done about as well as she had.

In the afternoon, as Sandra had anticipated, the competitions were some of the most fun – at least for the other contestants. Sandra's afternoon was loaded with problems. First up was cookie baking. She had decided on her "Island Granola Bars." She knew the bars wouldn't be quite as sweet as some of the other more standard Christmas cookie choices, but she felt like that might give her a slight edge by standing out to the judges. Her granola bars were both delicious *and* nutritious with flakes of coconut, chunks of nuts and bits of dried tropical fruit featured in every chewy bite. She felt certain both Santa and the reindeers would enjoy them. Right now, though, she just needed to be sure the bars were a treat enjoyed by the seven elf judges.

She had made these bars dozens of times, which helped her feel relaxed in the mini kitchen that had been set up for each contestant. When the buzzer went off indicating time was up, she presented her bars with pride, noting how pretty they were with their bits of fruit and nuts showing off like ornaments on a Christmas tree. Pride quickly faded to horror, though, as one by one the judges began spitting and sputtering after biting into her special granola bar creation and grabbing for their big glasses of water! Since she had made them so many times and was running short on time, Sandra had not tasted the bars before she presented them. Now, as the platter passed her way and she took a bite from one of her bars – which looked and smelled delicious – she knew the judges were right. They were awful! The only thing you could taste in them was salt.

"But there's no salt in the recipe," she said bleakly. "Salt must have been in the sugar container." When the judges checked the sugar container, however, it was only full of sugar.

Besides Sandra's salty gaggers, Nicholas Navidad burnt his cookies badly, complaining that his oven ran way too hot for 350 degrees. The other contestants, though, including Gunny, presented cookie wonders. Gunny baked up a cookie he called "Texas Christmas Stars." Redson did round cookies he called "Pots of Christmas Gold." Rollo made "Snowballs" and Klondike Tannenbaum did three- dimensional Christmas trees with an edible twinkling star at the top. Sandra couldn't believe how intricate they were for the short amount of time they had. From the look on the judge's faces, every cookie but hers was a luscious bite of lip-smacking goodness. One judge ate two of each.

Tree decorating was next up and Sandra knew she needed to rebound from the granola bar disaster. Each contestant was sequestered in a small room with walls on three sides and a closed curtain to the front. Sandra had decided to go with a tropical theme for her tree and had talked with the Tree Decorating

Assistance Committee members on the first day about what kinds of ornaments and lights she wanted for her tree. There were clear requirements on how the tree had to be decorated. It had to hold between 150 and 200 ornaments and be decorated with 800 to 1000 Christmas lights. It was a lot but the trees they had available were beautiful, bushy, tall evergreens that could hold a lot. The type of ornaments and lights, however, was left up to each contestant as well as any theme. The committee members had gotten Sandra the lights and ornaments that she had requested. For some reason, however, perhaps because she had requested tropical-themed ornaments, they had not given her one of the beautiful, tall, fir trees. Instead she had a tall palm tree with just a few fronds to decorate! She pulled the curtain back to inquire about the tree mix-up, but no one was anywhere around in the empty room to ask. She looked at the tree, the pile of lights and ornaments, the clock ticking fast on the wall and decided, especially after the cookie fiasco, she'd better make the best of it and make her tree shine. She decided maybe everyone's tree was different than they expected as part of the challenge.

She did her best to make the tree look cheery and fit everything required on it, but in the end, it looked a lot like a little girl who had gotten into her mother's makeup – it was overdone. Nonetheless, before she was finished, she plopped a bright-colored, stuffed parrot right at the top. "There you go, Squawk," she said to no one but herself. She stepped back and decided she liked her Christmas palm tree despite it's having way too much going on. The buzzer sounded, ending the round, and the curtains on each contestant's room opened for the judges to review.

All of the contestants stepped out away from their trees and were seated where they could view them all. Sandra saw that all the others had fir trees that now glowed in their Christmas finery. Redson had selected a "Lucky Charm" theme for his tree, complete with a pot of gold underneath it and a rainbow at the top. Gunny went with a sports theme. Rollo's looked like a mini version of the toy assembly department at the factory. Nicholas had gone with a sunshine theme similar to Sandra's tropical theme but used a tall evergreen tree topped with a sombrero. Klondike had done a stunning rendition of a traditional Christmas tree without a clear theme. After looking at them all, Sandra decided, next to hers, she liked Redson's best. As the judges walked up to judge his tree, the lights on it suddenly went out.

"Hey, what's happening?" the dismayed contestant exclaimed, jumping up from where he was sitting. He checked to see that the lights were plugged in and the plug was working. When he tested a spare string, it lit up but, no matter how much he jiggled and fussed with the lights on his tree, they wouldn't come back on.

Assembling simple toys was the next activity of the day, and one Sandra approached with an equal mix of determination and apprehension. Each contestant was given a big bag of toy parts and had one hour to assemble anything they wanted. At the end of the hour, Sandra had made a small model of Santa's sleigh. *Not bad*, she thought – until she saw what the others had done in the same amount of time. Gunny had put together a skier that moved. Redson had assembled a rainbow that lit up. Klondike had a nutcracker that really cracked nuts. Nicholas had a clever spinning piñata and Rollo, the master toy maker, had made an elf figurine that looked remarkably like himself. When you pulled a string, the figurine said, "Pick me, Santa" in Rollo's voice!

Gift-wrapping was the last event of the day, and the only shot that Sandra had left to bounce back at all. This time, the contestants were each given an assortment of mostly odd-shaped gifts to wrap and place under their Christmas trees. They all had access to a room of wrap and novelty items.

Sandra stuck with her tropical theme and used bright paper and fabrics to make her gifts look like oversized fruit. There was a banana, a pineapple, a coconut and a papaya. Then she wrapped the remaining boxed gifts in beach towels she had found on one of the shelves amongst the novelty items. She put everything under the tree, donned some sunglasses and got comfortable in a canvas chair that reminded her of a beach chair at home, to wait for the judges.

Fortunately, this time, it appeared she did well. For one thing, the guys – all of them – seemed to be pretty lousy at wrapping. Just as importantly, though, her daring originality finally seemed to be appreciated. She thought her packages looked festive with her over-decorated palm tree. Looking at it all made her lonesome for her island home.

Little did she know her home wasn't being decked out with Christmas lights like normal at this time of the year. Instead, it was being flattened out by wind.

Chapter 29

Jason and the Cave

Location: Cassandra Cay in the Hoppers

The group working on his behalf on St. Annalise would have been surprised to learn that Jason was putting a special power to work as well. They would have been surprised, because none of them knew Jason had any powers. Jason, being Jason, for his own moody reasons had never bothered to tell them or show them differently.

Once in the cave Jason practiced one of his recently discovered talents and made his hands glow with a kind of greenish hued light. He had discovered this new "power" by accident one day when Christina had asked him to get something out of the mansion basement and the light switch wasn't working. He simply had thought about how much he needed a light and his hands glowed. Just like that. It scared him at first and then he decided it was plain ole cool. He'd been practicing "hand lighting," as he'd taken to calling it, ever since. Still, for reasons even he wasn't sure about, he hadn't mentioned it to anyone. Not even Christina. Only Mango knew.

The glow emanating from Jason's hands showed they were in a small cave, about twelve feet around, he estimated. It had an opening to what seemed to be another cave at the back. The glow from his hands gave off light but it didn't give off any heat. The storm had brought an unusual cold temperature with it, and he knew he and Mango needed a fire to warm up and dry out. He was able to find enough scraps of twigs and driftwood in the first cave to build a small pile. When he was finished gathering what he could find, he lit some paper using a notepad and lighter he had in his backpack and soon had a decent-size fire going. It wouldn't last, though, unless he found more wood for it.

"C'mon, girl, let's get you warmed up," he said to his still shivering pet. He got her settled as well as he could and she quickly fell asleep. He took one of the longer pieces of wood that he had gathered and lit the end of it to make a torch. Now that he had the fire going, he didn't want to expend his energy making his hands glow if he didn't need the light. If they were going to stay warm, they'd need more fuel and he'd rather look in the second cave then go back out into the storm. Any wood he might have found out there would have been soaked anyway.

The little cave he and Mango were in was surprisingly dry and quiet, considering the storm that was raging just a few feet from them. He made his way to the back of it and held the torch through the hole. He couldn't see much past the torch light, but he could tell this second cave was much larger than the one they were in.

"Hello," he called out.

His hello echoed back to him.

"Anybody there?" he called out. "Any *thing* there?" he muttered to himself.

He heard only silence in response, so he tentatively stepped through the cave entrance and found himself not in simply a second cave – it was more like a cavern. He couldn't tell how far the space went back but he could hardly believe this big space was located under his tiny island. As his eyes adjusted and the torch lit the area around him and reflected off the wall and floor, he could see that the cave seemed pretty ordinary as far as caves go. It had a sandy floor and big boulders here and there but not much else. Unfortunately, he couldn't see any firewood, which meant he would have to push further into the dark space.

He moved slowly but steadily back. He kept close to one wall and began to notice that it had writing on it. *So I'm not the first person on this cay after all*, he thought. His imagination began to work overtime on who could have been there before him. He wondered if they might have been pirates. That almost seemed too good to be true to a rebel sort of guy like him.

He looked at the writing on the wall closer to see if it resembled any kind of treasure map, but it really didn't, he decided. Nor was the writing in any language he understood. For the first time ever, he wished he had paid more attention in his language classes. The thought made him smile . . . so did the huge pile of wood he had just spied.

It was actually logs and driftwood jumbled together in a big heap next to one of the boulders. He moved over to it and placed his torch in the sand for light about halfway between the pile and the opening to the smaller cave. Then he began tugging, pulling and pushing at the mound of driftwood, working pieces loose and placing them in a small pile close to the opening of the first cave. The torch provided just enough light for him to walk easily back and forth. As he was working hard at breaking off a particularly large chunk of one log, the hair on the back of his neck went up. Someone was whispering behind him! He whirled around.

"Who's there?" he said running to grab the torch and point it toward where he heard the whispering was coming from. "I said 'who's there?'" he said again louder and much braver then he felt. There was only silence. Was it the wind? Maybe, but it still creeped him out. It didn't sound like wind.

He looked at his pile of wood and decided he had plenty. He only had one more thing he wanted to do before he moved back to the comfort of the first, smaller cave. He pulled a notepad and pencil from his backpack and moved back over to the writings on the cave wall.

Even though it didn't look like a treasure map, it "doesn't mean it isn't" he said out loud, taking comfort in hearing his own voice. He tried to copy it carefully into his notepad. He wanted to get out of the big cavern but he needed to take his time and be accurate with what he wrote down. He was almost done when something dark flew out of the deep, black part of the cavern and swooped down on him!

"Hey!" he yelled, grabbing the torch and shaking it at the... bat? As it circled back around to dive at him again, he could see in the torch light that it wasn't a bat. In fact, he wasn't sure what it was. It seemed like it might be some kind of big dark bird like a raven but it had an oversized head. It cast a dragon-like shadow on the cave walls. "Hey!" Jason yelled again at it waving his torch. "Get out of here!" The apparent bird paid him no attention and proceeded to dive again at Jason, looking him in the eye. As it got right above him, Jason heard, "Don't come back here, Jason Annalise," and it dropped something on his shoulder!

"What the.." Jason stammered, stunned by what the bird had done and said. The flying offender was headed to the entrance of the cave and Jason ran after it. He got to the opening just as it flew out the first cave and into the wild storm. Mango had slept through it all.

Jason looked at his shoulder and saw the bird had soiled his jacket. The droppings had actually burned a hole in the material. Had he really heard, "Don't come back here, Jason Annalise?" He was certain he had. Or maybe not. He knew only one thing for sure. Whether he had or he hadn't heard it, no big, black, flying thing was going to keep him from coming back to Cassandra Cay to decipher the wall and see what else might be hiding in that cave. Like maybe a chest full of treasure for instance. Oh yea, he was coming back.

CHAPTER 30

Day Four Finals

Location: The North Pole

Sandra had stayed up late to practice her Christmas magic, work on levitation and spend some time with the reindeer. She woke up late and tired. "Not a good start to this busy day," she said to her reflection in the bathroom mirror as she scrambled to get ready. There was only one item on the schedule today but it was the big one: The Obstacle Course. This was the day that took everything they had learned so far and put it into a mini version of what happens on Christmas Eve.

After a quick goodbye to Cappie, even knowing they weren't going to be good, Sandra headed to take a look at the scores before she headed to Happiness Hall.

Day Three Competition Results

Cookie Baking – High Score:

Two-Way Tie – Redson O'Brien & Rollo Kringle

Tree Decorating – High Score:

Two-Way Tie – Klondike Tannenbaum & Nicholas Navidad
Toy Assembly – High Score:
Two-Way Tie – Rollo Kringle & Gunther Holiday
Gift Wrapping – High Score:

Cassandra Claus…

Cassandra frowned seeing her name listed just the once. She knew things hadn't gone well, but she had hoped it would be different.

"Hey, it's the master gift wrapper," Gunny greeted her and then saw the look on her face. "What's the matter this morning? Eat one of your own granola bars?"

"Real funny, Gunny," she said smiling at him and her own silly pun. "Are you ready for today?"

"Ready to win," he replied.

"Me, too," she said as they entered the hall and joined the other candidates who were already there.

"See you at the finish line."

"Okay, good, we now have everyone here," said an elf named Alexander who was lead on giving directions this morning and started in as the two joined the others. "I've got lots to cover before you can get started on your last event. I'll try to be thorough.

"Today, your task is to complete a five-step obstacle course.

"First, you will each be given a partial copy of 'The List.' This List has been put together featuring only volunteer children located right here at the Pole. Using the short descriptions provided, you must decide which children have been naughty and which children have been nice. I will provide you with a clue: only one child on each list has been naughty." Alexander looked at each candidate as if he had done them a really big favor before he continued on.

"Once you have evaluated your list, you then move to the toy inventory area, for step two. There you will select what gifts you wish to deliver and load them into your Santa bag."

Gunny and Sandra looked at each other and he shrugged his shoulders.

"For step three, you head straight to the reindeer barn. You will all be using the light-weight express sleighs today that only require two reindeer each. You will draw names for the reindeer. Because we have six contestants, we will be using Comet, Cupid, Zeus, Marty, Donner, Blitzen, Roman, Dasher, Dancer, Vixen, Apollo and Zanzibar. They are all fully trained in gift delivery and looking forward to assisting you. Prancer and Rudolph are not available for this exercise today – they're helping Santa with some practice runs. At the barn, you will load your sleighs and harness your reindeer."

Sandra looked at Gunny. "Sounds exciting, doesn't it?"

He put his finger to his lips. "Shhh, I want to hear what else he has to say." She grimaced at him in response to being shushed.

"You are now ready for gift delivery as the fourth step. For this, you need to use your reindeer training to remember stable lift-offs and landings. We encourage you to work to keep your sleigh steady to reduce the risk of any gifts falling out."

Sandra hoped she had practiced enough.

Alexander continued. "Use the Santa GPS installed in each sleigh to locate the homes of the children on your list. To save time, try to pick the most expedient route. When you land, remember that your goal is to land unnoticed," he paused for emphasis before moving on. "Then select the gifts for that home, pop down the chimney and set the gifts under the tree. Don't forget to tuck in some stocking stuffers and enjoy any cookies left out for you."

"Those cookies gave Santa that jelly belly," whispered Sandra. "I'll be hoping for some fruit slices or granola bars."

"Oh brother," Gunny whispered back, rolling his eyes. "You're really way too talkative today."

". . . then you pop back up the chimney, preferably by levitation but by reindeer-assisted-lift if necessary," Alexander said, giving a look at Sandra and Gunny for talking. "Once there, push off and head to the next home. Complete your task at each home on your list and head to the barn. At the barn, you check in with Barney, unharness your reindeer and get them back into the stall.

"Your last stop is to walk – or run – to North Pole Park, ring the park bell and celebrate your completion with all of us there waiting for you!"

Alexander paused for a minute, looking over his notes, before adding, "This is a timed event, but also important to the overall results will be your accuracy and quality level of service. Now, are there any questions? Yes, Nicholas?"

"Are all of the homes located here at the Pole?"

"Excellent question. Yes, they are all here; however, some temporary homes have been set up in areas on the perimeter of the Pole strictly for this exercise. There will be families staged in them. Additionally, some children may be located in apartments and condo units just as they would be in actual delivery circumstances."

"Is there anything else," he asked scanning the group. No one spoke up. "Alright then, this is it, everyone. You have all been the exceptional candidates that Santa and the selection committee believed you to be. Good luck today! I'll see you at North Pole Park!"

Chapter 31

The Big Finale

Location: The North Pole

All six of the contestants were uncharacteristically quiet as they filed out to collect their lists and make their toy selections. Each individual was assigned to a separate area at the village for their deliveries. Sandra studied the children on her list and quickly determined what child should be placed on the bad list. Like before, however, she simply couldn't make herself put him there, even though he clearly wasn't as well behaved as he should have been. Still, she felt he deserved a little something. She knew it would slow her down a bit, but she decided she would deliver gifts to each child. She needed to get busy selecting the toys so she could make up some of the time.

What fun she had picking out perfect presents for the children! She could hardly wait to slip each gift under their Christmas trees. At the last minute, she remembered to select things for stocking stuffers as well, packed it all in a big bag and headed to the barn where she saw she was arriving right behind Rollo and Gunny and ahead of the others.

She'd gotten Comet and Apollo in the reindeer drawing. They both snorted and stomped when she came into their stall. "I'm happy to see you both this morning, too," she said affectionately patting them on the head. Both reindeer cooperated as she harnessed and hooked them up to one of the express sleighs. So far so good, she thought, as she took the reins. Now if she could just get a smooth lift-off. "Up, up and away," she called out to the two reindeer with as much confidence in her voice as she could muster.

To her joy, the sleigh lifted off smoothly and they were airborne. She called out directions for the first stop.

The first home was located close to the arena. It was small with a short, wide chimney that she slipped down easily.

She sorted through her gift bag, found the gifts for the three children, filled their stockings, ate two bites out of the cookies and made it up the short chimney on her second try. "Next house, boys, let's move," she said to Comet and Apollo, feeling good about the first.

At the second house though, everything changed. It was a condominium unit with no chimney. Despite one of the lessons being on magically fabricating temporary chimneys and fireplaces, she hadn't excelled at it and frankly didn't like it. Still, she cast the Christmas magic and watched as a very small chimney appeared.

This is frustrating, she thought. *Even an elf couldn't get down that. If I'm an elfin princess why didn't I get any special powers?* Instead, there she sat. On a roof with two reindeer, a ridiculously small chimney before her and deserving children inside who wouldn't get any gifts because she wasn't good at Santa magic.

"It breaks my heart to disappoint them," she said frustratingly, out loud to no one really but herself after numerous tries to increase the temporary chimney size. "Oh Mom," she said reaching automatically to hold her locket as she did whenever she was stressed. "Why couldn't I have been as special as you?" She looked down in distress and saw now that her locket was glowing. It was glowing! Like it must have been that day in the paint vat. She knew it. When she looked close, she saw it said "wish."

"Wish?" she read out loud. "I wish I were inside this home" she said and then she was. She was! Just like that. She couldn't believe it. She had held the locket, wished for something from her heart and, just like that, it had come true.

"Thanks Mom!" she called out knowing that she had just experienced some kind of special elfin magic help. She had no time to think about it. She would have to figure out the how's and why's later because right now she still had to win this competition. She delivered her gifts, had some cookie bites, held her locket and wished to be back on the roof. It worked at all four of the remaining houses – even the home of the boy on the naughty list. She had left him a small remote-controlled car and taken the time to leave a note reminding him to be nice to his friends and teachers.

Even though she suspected the delay at the second house and extra stop had put her behind, Sandra still thought she might be ahead of a couple of the others, thanks to the magic of her locket. Until, that is, she got to the barn and saw that all the other reindeer were already there. Last! She came in last. She landed Comet and Apollo and sat there for a few minutes.

At this point, it hardly seemed important that she hurry to the park and she wanted to savor the time she had left at the Pole. She also wanted to work through her disappointment by herself before she faced the others. Rollo or Gunny was sure to be the person Santa selected and she could be happy for either one of them. She just needed to let go of her own dream first.

"squawk . . . there you are . . . squawk"

"Squawk!" she exclaimed. "What are you doing here? Is that really you? How'd you get here?" Sandra now bounded out of the sleigh to where her beloved parrot perched on the reindeer stall.

". . . flew . . . had to come . . . had some fairy help . . . trouble at home . . . big trouble . . . squawk . . . cold here . . ."

"What do you mean by trouble, Squawk?" Sandra asked now alarmed.

". . . big storm . . . damage . . . bad . . . Jason gone . . ."

"Jason's gone? Where'd he go?"

". . . don't know . . . don't know . . . blown away . . . just gone . . ."

"Is everyone else all right? Birdie? Spence? Christina? Thomas? Everyone?"

". . . yes . . . good . . . big mess . . . big mess . . . everyone hiding . . . big wind . . . little wind . . . Squawk came . . . find Sandra . . ."

As important as it had been, everything about the North Pole and being South Pole Santa fell away for Sandra, thinking about the trouble at St. Annalise. Her locket was still glowing and she knew how to get there fast.

"Squawk, hang on to me. We're going for a fast ride home."

"squawk . . . by sleigh?"

"Nope," she said smugly. "By locket."

" . . . leave a note . . . squawk . . . leave a note . . ."

"You're right, Squawk."

Sandra used a pen and paper she found on Barney's small desk and wrote out a quick note to Cappie. She put it in Comet's stall where she knew someone would find it. She also knew Cappie and Santa would be unhappy with her, but she'd have to deal with that later. She hated to miss the ball and the South Pole Santa announcement but she knew where she belonged. She needed to help find Jason.

She stepped to the front of the stall, Squawk flew to her shoulder, and she grasped her locket.

"Hang on, Squawk. I wish to be home please. To St. Annalise as fast as you can take us."

Chapter 32

Here, There and Everywhere

Location: St. Annalise Island

The duo set down on a quiet part of the beach just as dawn was breaking. The storm had moved on but not before it had blown much of St. Annalise into small pieces.

"Oh Squawk, it's a mess everywhere." She didn't even look over toward where the *Mistletoe* should be. What if it had been destroyed?

"C'mon, Squawk, let's go find everyone."

It took Sandra longer to get to the school than it did Squawk. Flying was a real advantage in a mess like this. He could avoid the chaos while she had to work her way around downed trees, outdoor furniture and pieces of the school roof. Before she got to the front door, Birdie and Spence and the others had spotted her from the cafeteria windows and came running out to greet her.

"Sandra! You're back! How'd you get here?"

"Squawk was very brave and came and got me," she said about her beaming bird and avoiding their direct question. "Is everyone okay? Is Jason back?"

"He's still missing," Birdie said shaking her head. "Thomas and some of the other boats headed out early today to look for him. Everyone else is okay but not really good." She looked glumly at her friend before continuing. "No one has any powers! For some reason, the storm, because it was really strong with so much thunder and lightning we're thinking, knocked out everyone's special powers. Nothing anyone has tried has worked to find Jason. Even now that it's passed, we still don't have our powers back. Sandra, I can't even understand most of the birds!" And she burst into tears. Spence stood there looking like he, too, was in a state of despair.

"Oh Birdie, it's going to be okay, really it will," Sandra said, comforting her best friend and reaching out to pull Spence in. "I know everything will come back as soon as the last of this horrible weather has passed."

The friends stood there for a moment looking at the destruction around them before Sandra finally asked what she needed to know even though she feared the answer. "Is the *Mistletoe* okay?"

"I'm sorry, Sandra," Birdie sniffled and used her sleeve to wipe the tears out of her eyes as Sandra dropped to her knees taking in the terrible news about the only home she'd ever known.

"Oh, no, no, Sandra!" Birdie said hastily after she looked quizzically at her friend on the ground until it dawned on her why Sandra was looking so devastated. "I meant, I'm sorry but none of us have checked down by the docks yet."

Hope surged in Sandra at those words! She gave Birdie a hug, squeezed Spencer's hand and headed to the wharf area to find out for herself. If the *Mistletoe* was afloat and in one piece, she was taking it out to help look for Jason. If no one's magical powers were working, then the good old-fashioned ways of searching were going to have to be good enough. He was alive and out there, she could feel it.

"Sandra, wait!" called out Christina, running past the rest of the group that was increasing in numbers on the beach. "Can you take out the *Mistletoe* and look for Jason? Thomas and the others are looking east – will you go west? How about checking out the Hoppers?"

Sandra nodded and headed out not wanting to explain that was already her plan. As she ran as fast as she could over and around the clutter that was strewn everywhere, she realized that no one had even thought to ask if she had won the competition.

CHAPTER 33

Finding Jason

Location: St. Annalise Island

"Hooray!" Sandra exclaimed as she spotted the wharf. She turned and gave a thumbs-up wave to the others she had left as reassurance.

Indeed, the *Mistletoe* and the other boats had weathered the storm well. Tugboats are built low and sturdy and made to last. Her decks were strewn with palm fronds and garbage, and the main window in the top wheelhouse had been blown out. It made for a total mess but it was all fixable. The important thing was her home was still afloat. Sandra felt relief wash over her. Her friends and the *Mistletoe* were okay. Now they needed to find Jason. She didn't bother picking anything up. She just untethered and set off. Birdie and Spence flew up the dock and jumped on the *Mistletoe's* deck just in time.

"Not without us," said Spence.

"I can't believe we didn't ask you how things went at the Pole," Birdie said immediately. "We were just so surprised to see you and it's been crazy here. I hope you'll forgive us."

"Oh, Birdie, I know, and, of course, I do," Sandra said, knowing she was just feeling sorry for herself earlier when they didn't ask. "I'll tell you guys all about it later. For now, the only thing that really matters is that I didn't win and I'm glad to be home."

"Where's Cappie?" Spence asked.

Good question, thought Sandra. "She should be home later today. I came ahead with Squawk."

"I can't believe you didn't win," Birdie said, glancing over at Spence. "Did you have fun?"

"It was the best time ever."

The *Mistletoe* was headed west to the Hoppers. Some of the Hoppers were just huge rocks while others were respectable-sized islands. No one but Jason went out to the area much. Even the closest of the chain of islands was an hour from St. Annalise for most boats, and there were surprisingly few places in the archipelago that had any good scuba or snorkel areas. Only a handful of the islands were sandy – most were just big, dangerous, rocks. Sandra hoped they'd find the *Outcast* there in the Hoppers . . . just not smashed on one of the rocks.

The friends set out, monitoring the radio. Rio had joined them and Squawk was scouting out ahead. The three friends were sitting in the wheelhouse catching up on the past week when Squawk came flying back fast. He decided he liked having the wheelhouse window gone since it allowed him to fly straight in. He barely slowed down.

"Squawk, be careful!" Sandra scolded the bird. "You just about landed in Birdie's lap."

". . . squawk . . . Rio found Jason . . . squawk . . ."

"Rio found Jason? Where?" The babbling dolphin was now right off the port side of the boat, talking with Squawk.

". . . not Jason . . . Jason's boat . . ."

"Where, Rio?" Sandra asked the dolphin directly. "Take us to it."

Rio babbled some more dolphin and Squawk, acting as the official interpreter, shared, ". . . squawk . . . not far..."

Spence radioed the other boats to head for the Hoppers as Sandra steered the *Mistletoe,* trying to keep up with Rio. Even though most of the Hoppers were small, there were over a hundred of them that spread down a sea bed ridge for roughly 20 miles. Now they just had to find which one the *Outcast* had ended up on.

Chapter 34

Found!

Location: Cassandra Cay in the Hoppers

Jason and Mango had been stuck in the cave for almost five full days and nights, waiting for the storm to blow over. Fortunately, the food and water Jason had grabbed off the *Outcast* was enough to get them through the bleak time. Although he occasionally had paced around the small cave, most of the time the two had stayed huddled by the fire. Jason worked on studying the cave markings he had copied from the wall to pass the time. He couldn't decide if it was some kind of hieroglyphics or some kind of ancient pictorial language. He had returned to the bigger cave briefly each day for more firewood but had kept the visits short. Mango went with him each time. Despite her injured paw, she needed to get some exercise and he wanted the company. After the whisperings and the big bird thing, he was uneasy, even though he didn't see or hear anything else.

One night, though, Mango had woke him up, emitting a low growl. She was staring at the second cave opening. Jason couldn't make himself go look to see why. Instead, he built up the fire, lay back down and kept his eyes shut. That didn't mean he was asleep, however. Finally, the storm broke early the next morning, and the two were able to emerge from their hiding spot and make their way back to the *Outcast*.

Jason actually saw the *Mistletoe* in the distance before they got a look at him. He was making his way across the rocks, Mango limping beside him, when he saw a boat on the horizon and two more coming from the other direction. They were found! He didn't know how and he didn't care, he just wanted off this small speck of land. He wanted help for Mango, a hot shower, something to eat and some real rest for both of them.

As the first boat got closer, he could see it was the *Mistletoe.* The trio on board saw him walking the beach about the same time and started blasting the horn. "We found him!" was the message they sent out over the ship's radio. The *Mistletoe* dropped anchor and he saw the tugboat's dinghy making its way toward him with Sandra rowing.

Jason was confused to see it wasn't Cappie but Sandra. Why was she home already? That was the first thing he asked her when she hopped on to shore.

"Jason!" she waved at him. "You're safe! Everyone's been so worried. What happened to Mango?" She could see the dog's wrapped paw.

Jason ignored the question and her concern. He had a bad suspicion on why she was there. "What are you doing here, Sandra?" he asked too strongly. "How come you're back already?"

"I, I heard about the storm and you and..."

"Oh man, Sandra, we didn't need your help. You shouldn't have come. You shouldn't have left the Pole."

Despite the hurtful things he said, he was thrilled to see her and madder than he'd ever been. He knew she'd left the competition for him and he definitely wasn't worth it.

Now she was mad, too. *He was always so ungrateful*, she fumed to herself. She'd only just rushed back clear from the North Pole. "I didn't come for you. I came for everyone else and *they* made me come for you," she lashed back at him. "I didn't win anyway. Would it kill you to be just a little bit grateful? Where are we anyways?" she added as she looked around, anxious to change the subject.

"Just a cay in the Hoppers." He already felt bad for lashing out at her.

Sandra stood still, looking around at the small island. The island was prettier and bigger than most but there wasn't much of anything there to see except rocks and sand. She looked over at what was left of the *Outcast*.

"Rio's the one that found you. She saw the *Outcast*. How did you and Mango stay safe here through the storm?"

"I found a cave in the rocks over on the far side," Jason said more casually then he felt. Sandra was still scanning the island, now studying the area of the rocks.

"Jason, is there anyone else on this island with you?"

"Does it look like there is?" he asked sarcastically, wondering what kind of question that was.

"I don't know. I guess not but I could have sworn I saw something –" she said hesitantly still looking at the rocky area. "I'm glad you and Mango are safe. Can we go?"

"Will you take Mango with you? I want to wait for Thomas and the others to see if they think we can get the *Outcast* out of here or not."

Sandra looked at the wrecked boat doubtfully, back to Jason and out to where the other boats were now anchoring by the *Mistletoe.*

"Sure," was all she finally said, too tired to argue or even care anymore. *Stay here with your stupid little wrecked boat on this spooky little pretty island,* she thought. She took Mango from him and turned back to the dinghy to row back out to the *Mistletoe.* "See you back at St. Annalise," she called to him without looking back.

He watched the *Mistletoe* go. So did something else.

Chapter 35

Round Trip

Location: The North Pole

Cappie had waited at North Pole Park with the others for more than an hour after the rest of the candidates had arrived. Rollo had been the first in, followed by Gunny, then Redson, Nicholas and Klondike. Cappie knew Sandra would be disappointed that she came in last but Cappie wasn't dismayed at all. In her eyes, Sandra was always a winner.

Cappie's concern with Sandra being late turned to outright panic and anger, though, when Barney came running from the barn with the note Sandra had left.

Dear Cappie,

Jason is missing and St. Annalise has been hit by a big storm. I've gone to help. I have to, Cappie. Please tell Santa and the others (especially Gunny) thank you for me.

Love, Sandra

Gone from the Pole? Cappie had to read the note twice before it sank in. Gunny had waited at the park with her and he read the note as well.

"Who's this Jason guy?" he asked. "You know, never mind that. Let's go get her back."

Cappie nodded and asked Barney to take her to Santa.

Chapter 36

A surprise visitor

Location: St. Annalise Island

Once the other boats returned and Jason was safe, everyone on the island started right in on clean-up. The island had been hit hard. It was going to take weeks to get it all repaired, but everyone agreed it would have been much worse without the protection from the partial cloak the fairy students had managed to provide before their powers got knocked out. That was good news, too: everyone's magical powers and abilities seemed to be returning now that the storm was completely gone.

For the rest of the day, the group put hard work and magic together and made good progress on getting the main paths around the campus cleared of the worst of the mess. For Sandra, the long day had started at the Pole. It seemed a long time ago already, she thought, as she lay out on the *Mistletoe's* deck, exhausted, looking at the sky and thinking about the fun everyone must be having at the Christmas Cotillion dance. She wondered if the winner had been announced yet. She liked all the contestants but she hoped Gunny won, or Redson. They both made her laugh. Probably Rollo was the winner, though. He seemed to win most of the competitions.

South Pole Santa, she thought to herself. "South Pole Sandra," she said out loud giving it her own spin and enjoying the sound of it.

"Sounds kind of nice really," a voice said that gave her the biggest fright she thought she might have ever had. In one quick move, she went from lying down flat on her back to standing straight. Standing there behind her, glowing in the light of the full moon, was none other than Gunther W. Holiday the Fourth.

"Gunny?! You scared me! What are you doing here? How'd you get here? Why aren't you at the ball?"

"Whoa, whoa, whoa, Houdini. You pull a disappearing act like that and you're the one with all the questions?" he grinned at her as he sat down on the rail of the boat. She sat down next to him, grinning back at him.

"It's beautiful here, Sandra – even at night," he said, actually using her name for a change. "I can see why you love it." It could have been a nice special moment between them but Sandra had far too many questions for him.

"So c'mon, Gunny, talk to me. Is Cappie here? What happened after I left?"

"Oh you mean after you departed without a word to anyone? Well then your guardian was mad as a hungry polar bear. She went storming off to Santa to tell him what you'd done. After hearing about the situation here at your island and about your missing friend and all, Santa called the full Claus Council and all of the candidates together and asked if we would be willing to postpone the ball and the announcement to tomorrow night. Seems like the big guy has a lot of clout, 'cause everyone but me voted to wait." He grinned at her and she slapped him on the arm.

"Do you mean...are you saying...are you saying that the Cotillion and the announcement aren't happening till tomorrow night?"

He grinned and nodded, feigning like she might hit him in the arm again.

"And you came to get me?"

He nodded again.

"Hey, I had to. I mean I couldn't win without you there to cheer me on. Besides, the rest of the girls up there are all a little short for me to dance with, ya know."

"Oh, Gunny," she said and threw herself at him for a big hug – sending them both right over the edge of the boat and into the water!

As soon as they came to the surface, Gunny practically walked on water getting to the dock in his hurry to get out.

"Something just rubbed up against me and I'm telling you it wasn't you," said her hero.

"Gunny, its Rio," said Sandra laughing. The emerald green dolphin broke the surface and jabbered to Gunny directly. He just looked at her warily.

"Just tell her that where I come from, you get to know someone first before you nudge on 'em like that."

Sandra and Rio both grinned.

"Now, c'mon, as fun as this is, we gotta get going," he said, already climbing back into the boat. "Oh, and you can grab your friends too, this Birdie and Spence. Santa says they can come back with you this time if you want."

Santa had actually said Birdie, Spence *and* Jason but somehow Gunny forgot to tell her that part.

"They can go?" Sandra looked at him for confirmation and then went flying down the dock, dripping wet. She called back, "Go on in and dry off – there are towels and robes inside – you'll see them. Put a robe on and put your clothes in the dryer. I'll be back with Spence and Birdie in no time. If you need anything, ask Squawk." She raced off.

In the home he shared with Christina behind the academy, Jason had been doing some thinking of his own, mostly about what a jerk he had been. Sandra had come clear back from the North Pole, before the competition ended, just to help him, and he had been awful to her again. Even though it was late, he wanted to try and explain why, tell her about the cave and how glad he really had been to see her.

From shore, he could see there were still lights on the *Mistletoe* so he headed down the dock. When he got to the tug, he called out, "Sandra? You awake? Sandra?"

"'Fraid she's not here right now," said some guy in a robe that Jason had never seen. Gunny, however, figured out immediately that this had to be Jason.

"You must be Jason."

"Who are you?"

"Gunther Holiday the Fourth. She hasn't told you about me yet then? Ain't that just the way with women?"

Jason ignored his comment. He was completely thrown off by Gunny being there.

"Where is she?"

"She had to run and get some things from school before we headed back to the Pole."

"You mean she's going back?"

"She didn't tell you that either?" He let out a low whistle through his teeth.

Jason turned down the dock.

"I'll tell her you came by."

"Don't bother."

CHAPTER 37

The Dress

Location: The North Pole

Birdie and Spence couldn't believe they got to go back to the Pole with Sandra. Gunny had put the sleigh down behind one of the storage sheds near the beach and the friends squeezed in together. The trio laughed and told stories the whole way. Gunny and the reindeer got them back to the Pole with time to spare, and Cappie was there to greet them in front of the hotel.

While her two best friends exclaimed over all they were seeing at the village, like Sandra had done just a few days before, Sandra rushed to hug her guardian. "I'm sorry Cappie," she said.

"It's alright," Cappie replied. "Is everything okay at home? Did you find Jason? Is the *Mistletoe* in one piece?"

Sandra still didn't know Jason had come looking for her. Somehow, again, Gunny had forgotten to mention that to her during the last few hours on the express ride.

"Yes, we found him and everyone is doing alright. The *Mistletoe* made it."

"Did you bring Squawk back?" Cappie asked looking around.

"No. He said it was too cold, if you can believe that! He actually wanted to stay home."

"I'll see you in a few hours," Gunny said as he headed to the hotel doors. "Try to get a nap. That's what I'm hoping to do." He stifled a yawn.

"Thank you again, Gunny," Sandra gave him a quick, shy hug. "Good luck tonight," she added.

"You too, Island Girl."

All week Cappie had been working on the replacement dress for Sandra to wear to the cotillion. It had turned out to be as beautiful as the one Sandra had originally packed. The green and blue shimmery taffeta gown would set off Sandra's eyes perfectly.

"Cappie, it's beautiful," Sandra exclaimed as Cappie held the dress out to show it off.

"Thanks, honey. Would you mind if Birdie wore this tonight to the Cotillion?" Cappie asked a surprised Sandra who wondered what she would wear if Birdie got this beautiful dress.

"Are you kidding, Cappie? I get to wear this? No way!" Birdie exclaimed when she saw the gown.

"If it's okay with Sandra."

"It's okay with me Cappie, of course," Sandra said recovering from her surprise and seeing how excited Birdie was. "But what are you thinking I will wear? Did you find my other dress?"

"It's a surprise. Breezy is having it pressed – and I bet that's it right now," she added as someone knocked on the door.

Sure enough, a toy soldier was at the door, holding out his big uniformed arm, "Your dress, Captain Richmond."

It turned out that besides Sandra and her friends, Gunny had brought something else back from the *Mistletoe* that Cappie had requested – a dress for Sandra to wear to the ball.

Cappie turned from the door with not a dress really, more like an exquisite piece of art masquerading as a dress. It was a simple, white, form-fitting silk gown with pink see-through layers of a gossamer-like fabric laid over the silk. Each layer shimmered with a sparkle unlike anything Sandra had ever seen. The bodice of the dress captured most of Sandra's attention. It had a delicate embroidery design stitched into the dress, and at the center of it you could clearly see a round circle with three straight lines, that was the simple family insignia.

"Cappie, was this my mother's dress?" Sandra asked almost in a whisper.

"Yes," said Cappie beaming. "She wasn't that much older than you when she made it for a coronation ceremony." She didn't add that it had been for Cassieopola's own coronation ceremony.

Sandra instinctively knew that, though. "This is the most wonderful surprise you could have possibly given me," she said with tears in her eyes.

"Okay then, girls, no time for sentiment. It's time to get ready! Spence, your tux is in Gunny's room which is just down the hall."

They had to rush but everyone managed to get dressed in their best and be ready on time. Sandra had emerged from her dressing room looking like a princess out of a fairy tale. The dress fit as though it had been custom designed just for her. But it was her hair that took everyone's breath away. She wore it down and, for the first time ever in public, she let it sparkle. She had decided these were people she could, and would, trust. Cappie, Birdie and Spence, all looking beautiful themselves – stood staring at her.

"You guys," she said. "You're embarrassing me."

"How did you do that to your hair?" Spence finally asked.

"Oh, you know, Spence – we girls have our secret ways."

"Teach that to me some time, please," said Birdie, making Sandra feel slightly guilty since it couldn't really be taught. "Sandra, you look amazing."

"You do too, Birdie. You too Cappie. Even you, Spence," she added grinning.

Chapter 38

And The Winner Is . . .

Location: The North Pole

While everyone else around the Pole was busy getting dressed for the big night, the decorating committee members had been putting the final touches on Happiness Hall.

"Wow!" was the only word anyone used as they entered the space. The hall was beautiful before, but it had become magical now. The decorating committee had transformed it into the Northern Lights. Bands of colored lights flickered across the room just like the real Northern Lights. Tiny lights twinkled on the ceiling like stars. Each table glowed with giant glass snowflakes in the middle of white-on-white tablecloths and settings. The effect was breath-taking. So was Sandra.

As a competitor, Sandra entered the hall alone, as her name was announced. She felt pretty but she still was not prepared for the response to her entry. The whole of the hall gazed at her in a stunned silence and then broke into a respectful applause. It was a far different greeting then the first time she had been announced here.

It was Gunny's reaction, though, that she liked the best. For once, he was speechless. He stared at her from across the room and then walked toward her, never taking his eyes away, as people moved out of his way. *Like in a movie,* Sandra thought watching him.

"This magical hall," he said to her, sweeping his hand toward the room, "pales in comparison to how beautiful you are tonight.

"I thought being named South Pole Santa this evening would probably be the best memory of my life," he continued. "But now, now I think this moment, seeing you, might be the greatest."

Wow, thought Sandra, *now that's the way to talk to a girl.* At the same time she also thought he was awfully sure of himself. One of the other candidates – including her – still had a chance at being named South Pole Santa.

"Everyone here, including you, looks spectacular tonight," she replied sincerely, beaming as he escorted her to her table. Unlike the other contestants, Gunny hadn't brought anyone else along from home to the Pole for the competition. ("Nah, I'm more of a loner that way" he had said when Sandra had asked him.) They were able to squeeze a place setting for him onto their table when he asked one of the waiters to be moved. The group included Sandra, Cappie, Birdie, Spence, Breezy, Rumpus, Zinga, Zoomer and Gunny. Sandra felt she had the very best table.

What a night it turned out to be! Everyone enjoyed a seven-course dinner prepared by the best of the North Pole chefs. The best part was dessert! Of course, the elves all thought so but even the guests loved it. The dessert chefs prepared Flaming Baked Alaska – an ice cream and cake creation set on fire for drama – that was delivered to each table by dancing elves with Ellen leading the way.

There was a full orchestra that took requests. Sandra danced with all the contestants plus Spence and Birdie and even Santa for one rock-n-roll number. She twisted with Zoomer and led off a bunny hop line that the whole room joined in. The orchestra played carols, ballads, fast numbers, slow numbers and songs from around the world in honor of all the contestants. Gunny requested a country song Sandra had never heard, about "friends in small places" or something like that, and the crowd went wild. They all seemed to know how to country line dance but all she did was laugh through it when Gunny tried to teach her.

Every single person in the room seemed to be having a ball at the ball. Thank goodness she didn't miss it, Sandra thought between dances. Even without the South Pole Santa announcement, this was one very special night.

"May I have this dance?" Gunny asked for the fifth or sixth time that night. Gunny turned out to be a strong and skilled dancer. Her favorite dance of the night had been a German polka where Gunny whirled her around the room, literally sweeping her off her feet.

It was just before 11:00 PM when the North Pole Elf Drumline came marching into the hall. Announcement time had arrived! As the drummers performed, Santa took to the podium. Gunny squeezed her hand. She knew he wanted it – she wanted it for him – but not as much as she wanted it for herself.

"Ho Ho Ho!" Santa started, talking loudly to get everyone's attention. "Ho Ho Ho!" he said again. While the contestants and their guests were already quiet, it always took elves a little longer. He waited patiently for just a moment.

"Welcome, everyone, welcome. Hasn't this been a fantastic party? What a memorable night this already is," Santa said to everyone there. "I know you are all anxious to hear who has been selected as our new South Pole Santa, and I am eager to share the news with you. First, however, before I share that big news, I have a bit of unexpected business I must take care of with you all." Elf hubbub buzzed around the room. Elves get nervous about anything unexpected. "Hotshot, will you join me up here?" Santa said, looking toward the back of the room.

A rather smug-looking elf in a back corner of the room looked surprised to hear his name, and he slowly made his way to join Santa at the front. Some of the other elves along the way cheered him on. "Way to go, Hotshot! Wow, Hotshot!" The elf barely looked at them as he trudged reluctantly forward, taking each step slower than the one before.

"As part of our process," Santa continued when the pale-looking elf arrived to the podium. "I assigned 'guardians' to each of our contestants. It was imperative that nothing happened to any of our visitors while they were here. Additionally, I wanted an unbiased report on how each day was going." Santa looked over at Hotshot, who was biting his lip and staring at his shoes with intensity, before he continued.

"It took some time to figure out, but, thanks to the work of these appointed guardians, I'm afraid I have eye-witness accounts and photos that clearly show that our own Hotshot has been causing problems of various sorts for each of our candidates – except for Rollo."

The whole room took a collective gasp and moved from staring at Hotshot to glaring at Rollo. "Rollo!" they all seemed to gasp at once. Santa hurried on.

"Now, now, it turns out this has nothing to do with Rollo really. I spoke to him about it earlier this evening, and I believe him when he says he knew nothing about what was going on. I think that sabotaging the other candidates was something that Hotshot decided completely on his own in a misdirected belief that he would be helping Rollo to win. Hotshot," Santa turned to face the elf who looked like he might run, "is that right?"

The normally assured elf was swaying and his knees were visibly knocking together. It seemed at first he was going to deny it, before he nodded his head ever so slightly in agreement with what Santa had said.

"Well, for all of us, this is certainly unfortunate. I want to apologize to each of the contestants who have suffered things such as –" Santa paused as he looked at an apparent list in front of him and read directly from it "– stolen luggage, late wake-up calls, being hit by snowballs, bad directions, missing clothes, burnt cookies, salt in the sugar container, burned out light bulbs, this list goes on and on." Santa then turned his attention fully to Hotshot.

"Hotshot, really," Santa said looking frustratingly at the dejected elf. "Is there anything you would like to say to everyone here tonight?"

"Sorry," the pale elf mumbled. "Sorry" he said a little louder. "I didn't mean to hurt anyone. I just wanted Rollo to win really badly. That's all."

"Hotshot!" exclaimed Rollo. "I didn't need any help. I would only want to win fairly."

"We'll talk about this more after Christmas, Hotshot," Santa said to the now very dejected elf. "Until then, you are on barn clean-up duty and no more shenanigans. You can go."

"I promise, Santa. Sorry, everybody," the elf said again to the crowd as he scurried away from the stage much faster than he had moved to get on the stage.

Sandra could hardly believe it. That explained what happened to her dress and who hit her with the snowball rock in the park the first night. It even explained why her granola bars had been terrible. And maybe she was right about being pushed into the blue paint vat after all. But that was more than an inconvenient prank that day. She could have died. She shivered thinking about it.

"Wow, that was pretty messed up," Gunny whispered to her after the announcement while Santa helped Hotshot off the stage. "I think Hotshot's the one who kept making me late for the morning sessions, and I'll bet he's the reason your cookies were so awful."

"I told you there was salt in the sugar bin. Lucky for you, too. My granola bars would have won for sure!" Sandra said, laughing at the face Gunny had made at the mention of her granola bars. There was another drum roll from the elf band and Santa started again.

"Ho Ho Ho! And now these unpleasantries aside, despite this bit of trickery, or perhaps I should call it 'elfery,'" he paused to let the crowd enjoy his pun, "let's move on to the announcement we have all been waiting for. As you all surely remember, it was only a few weeks ago that we were faced with the pending crisis of the world population exceeding one Santa's ability to deliver gifts on time. It was then that our Claus Council came up with the solution to add another Santa.

"That very same day, our own Wicket suggested that we could locate him, or her," he said with a nod to Sandra, "at the South Pole. South Pole Santa. I liked it. I think we all like it. It was an excellent idea." Wicket was pleased with Santa's praise.

"Thank you very much, sir," Wicket said as his friends jostled him with praise.

"I think most of you have met each of our candidates by now and you know how tough a decision this has been. Each individual would make a fine South Pole Santa. Each of you" – and he made eye contact with each contestant before he went on – "are exceptional individuals that I would be honored to work with. But in the end, of course, I can select only one."

"Good luck, Sandra," Birdie whispered across the table to her best friend. Gunny shushed at her and Birdie glared at him.

"And now, without any further kind of delay, let me share with you, this history-making choice. I know you will all fully support who I have selected," Santa continued. "This individual scored well, as they all did really, in most of the competitions, but this person added something additional, something important, something often underappreciated." Sandra felt

Gunny sit up even taller in his chair. She glanced over at Rollo who was also beaming. *I wonder which one of them will get it?* she thought to herself.

"If you remember, I mentioned earlier that you each were accompanied every day by an appointed guardian," Santa was saying to the candidates directly. "Their job was to watch over you, make sure the rules were followed and take notes on how your days went. The report I received each day on this particular individual was the most positive. This candidate, time and again, throughout the week, demonstrated the importance of being nice, of being considerate, of being loyal and kind. That is the true spirit of Christmas and when everything else was equal between the candidates, those are the qualities that I looked most at to make my decision. I can teach you all how to make toys – how to wrap them, how to deliver them and the other mechanics of being a good Santa. What I can't really teach anyone is how to be sincerely nice, day in and day out, and why it matters. That comes from inside and is a part of who you are. Let me be clear, each of you here, each person in this hall in fact, is most often unselfish, generous and kind. This person, however, openly demonstrated those qualities frequently throughout the week." *I wonder what he did?* Sandra was thinking.

"And so, all of you gathered in Happiness Hall on this historic day, please join me in congratulating, if she chooses to accept – " he paused as the hall burst out in chattering everywhere. *Did he just say "she?"* raced through Sandra's head as the world started to spin. She struggled to focus on what Santa was saying because surely she wasn't hearing it right and if she was, she wanted to hear every word.

"...Cassandra Penelope Clausmonetsiamlydelaterra..., most recently of St. Annalise Island, as our new South Pole Santa!"

With that, every single, somewhat stunned, person in Happiness Hall, even the other disappointed candidates and their guests, stood up and broke into cheers of congratulations and loud applause. Every person, that is, except Gunny, who, when she looked to see what he thought, was no longer at the table. She looked around for him but instead found Cappie and her friends, and a hundred other people who closed in all at once to congratulate her.

"Cappie, we did it!" she said in disbelief, hugging her guardian. "We did it!"

"My precious one – you did it," Cappie said beaming with the kind of love and pride reserved for parents and those that love you the most.

"Sandra you did it! You did it!" Birdie and Spence screamed in unison.

"Congratulations, Cassandra," Santa's voiced boomed as he made his way to her through the crowd. "We'll start training tomorrow. For now, can I have this next dance? Orchestra, give us one of your best. We have big news to celebrate!"

Chapter 39

Work, Work, Work

Location: The North Pole

The dream of being South Pole Santa turned into the work of being South Pole Santa the very next day. Christmas Eve was only a week away and there was so much to be done – more than most years. The Santa competition had been a distraction for everyone and toy production had fallen behind.

Cappie, Birdie and Spence volunteered to stay on to help as did the other South Pole Santa contestants. Everyone got assigned to specific tasks and Sandra worked directly with Santa.

Each day started with reviewing The List. For Sandra, this was her least favorite job. She always wanted to put every child on the Nice List. Santa would frown at her over his glasses, but he increasingly ended up agreeing with her and their Naughty List was growing shorter every day. On the other hand, she had decided that her favorite activity so far was reading the letters that children from around the world wrote to Santa.

Each letter was packed full of personality! Some children sent long lists, some sent short. Some children asked about life at the North Pole, others sent letters tattling on their sister or brother. Sandra's favorites were the ones that sent drawings. She also liked the letters that were written in languages she didn't get to use much because they gave her some needed practice. She was looking forward to the day when some of them, she hoped, would be addressed to South Pole Santa.

After lunch, the two studied Santa's geography maps. Wicket would join them to point out some of the more remote areas. One of the biggest challenges was locating children. Some people moved a lot! After a short dinner break, Santa had Sandra study with a variety of personal elf tutors for hours in the evenings. She practiced levitation, sleigh driving, using Christmas magic dust, stocking stuffing and languages. Thank goodness the North Pole had longer days so they could get it all done. She would drag her tired self back to the hotel each evening for a late night cocoa with Cappie and her friends in the hotel dining room and then drop like a rock into bed.

One evening after a light dinner with Cappie in their room, Sandra fell asleep on the couch exhausted from her schedule. She often dreamed when she was the most tired and on this night found herself on the *Mistletoe* in the middle of a beautiful blue sea on a sunny day. As she lay there relaxing and enjoying the warm sun on her skin, she smelled the unmistakable fragrance of her mother's perfume. Sitting up straight on the deck, she breathed in deeply and the aroma brought back how much she missed her. Tears filled her eyes.

Though she didn't talk about it much, she still missed her parents every day and wished, more than ever, that they could be with her to share in her success. In her dream, her mother's voice was talking to her.

"Cassandra, we're here."

"Mom! Where are you? Why can't I see you?"

"Your father and I are in the same place as we always are – all around you."

"I miss you and Dad so much. I have so much to tell you! Something big happened to me! I'm the new South Pole Santa, Mom. Oh Oh Oh! Isn't that great?"

"We're so proud of you, our wonderful, kind, daughter. You are more than we ever dared hope for in a daughter. Talk to us whenever you want, we'll always listen."

"I miss you so much that I think I can't stand it sometimes, Mom."

Her mother's voice was a gentle, fading, whisper. "We know sweetheart, we know. We love you, Cassandra. Take care of the ring . . ."